# Christmas Cake

Center Point
Large Print

Also by Lynne Hinton
and available from Center Point Large Print:

*Wedding Cake*

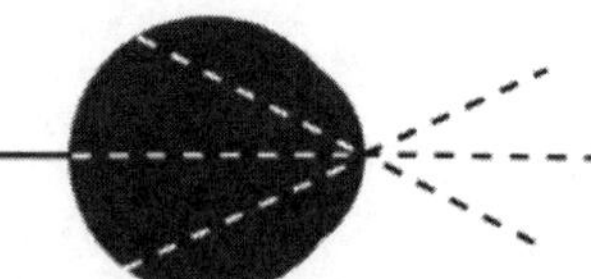

**This Large Print Book carries the Seal of Approval of N.A.V.H.**

# Christmas Cake

LYNNE HINTON

CENTER POINT PUBLISHING
THORNDIKE, MAINE

This Center Point Large Print edition
is published in the year 2010 by arrangement with
Avon Books, an imprint of HarperCollins Publishers.





The text of this Large Print edition is unabridged.
In other aspects, this book may vary
from the original edition.
Printed in the United States of America
on permanent paper.
Set in 16-point Times New Roman type.

ISBN: 978-1-60285-935-7

Library of Congress Cataloging-in-Publication Data

Hinton, J. Lynne.
Christmas cake / Lynne Hinton.
p. cm.
ISBN 978-1-60285-935-7 (library binding : alk. paper)
1. Female friendship—Fiction 2. Church membership—Fiction
3. North Carolina—Fiction. 4. Cookery—Fiction. 5. Large type books. I. Title.
PS3558.I457C47 2010
813′.54—dc22

2010026675

Dedicated to the memory of
Glenda Belvin Andrews
and
Frances Holt

# Acknowledgments

Every writer knows she relies upon the support, encouragement, and assistance of many people. First, I am grateful to my husband, always the true champion of my writing. I'm thankful for Sally McMillan, friend and agent, who works tirelessly on my behalf. I am happy to be back with HarperCollins and I wish to say thank you to Wendy Lee for standing behind this book and to Eleanor Mikuchi for her very keen eye in her work as copy editor.

Sylvia Belvin furnished the recipes. Mount Hope UCC brought me the community of Hope Springs. Isabella Valcarcel helped me with Spanish. St. Paul's UCC gave me room to write. And many loved ones created the foundation for this story which is true friendship.

I am blessed in so many ways and I am grateful for every day of my life. Thank you to everyone who keeps me centered and who loves me. Thank you for every act of kindness. Thank you to everyone who makes my life as sweet as cake.

# Cake Recipes

# SECTION ONE

❄❄❄

## *It's a Contest!*

The Cookbook Committee of the Hope Springs Community Church is holding a Christmas Cake Recipe Contest. The winner will receive a very special prize and will be the honored selection in the Hope Springs Community Holiday Cookbook. For more details, contact Bea Witherspoon, Louise Fisher, Jessie Jenkins, or Margaret Peele.

# Holiday Party Cake

❄❄❄

⅔ cup butterscotch morsels
¼ cup water
2¼ cups sifted all-purpose flour
1 teaspoon salt
1 teaspoon baking soda
½ teaspoon baking powder
1¼ cups sugar
½ cup shortening (part butter may be used)
3 eggs
1 cup buttermilk or sour milk

Melt butterscotch morsels in water in saucepan. Let cool. Sift flour with salt, baking soda, and baking powder; set aside. Add sugar gradually to shortening, creaming well. Blend in eggs; beat after each. Add butterscotch; mix well. Add dry ingredients alternately with buttermilk. Blend well after each addition. Bake in greased and floured 9 x 13–inch pan at 375 degrees for 25 to 30 minutes. Cool. Frost with sea foam icing.

[*continued*]

## SEA FOAM ICING

⅓ cup sugar
⅓ cup firmly packed brown sugar
⅓ cup water
1 tablespoon corn syrup
1 egg white
¼ teaspoon cream of tartar

Combine in a saucepan the sugar, brown sugar, water, and corn syrup. Cook until a little syrup dropped in cold water forms a soft ball (236 degrees). Meanwhile, beat egg white with cream of tartar until stiff peaks form. Add syrup mixture to egg white in slow steady stream, beating constantly until thick enough to spread.

# Chapter One

"It's just the name of the cake," Louise noted to Beatrice, who was complaining about the opening recipe in the new holiday cookbook the Women's Guild at Hope Springs Community Church was putting together.

At the last meeting, late in the month of October, the evening after Margaret kept her doctor's appointment, the committee had agreed to carry out Beatrice's plan for a cake recipe contest to find and name the new Hope Springs Community Christmas Cake as well as create a cake cookbook.

"It's called a party cake, Louise, a party cake," she said with emphasis. "It just doesn't sound good. It shouldn't be the opening recipe for our holiday cookbook. It gives a bad first impression."

"Holiday party cake," Louise corrected her.

"What?" Beatrice asked.

"The correct name is holiday party cake. And I don't see what's wrong with it. The recipe is harmless. The cake is harmless. You can belong to a church and still have a party."

Beatrice blew out a breath. "That's not the point."

Louise waited. When her friend didn't go on, she asked the obvious question.

"Okay, what is the point?"

Beatrice leaned against her counter in the kitchen. She was slowly cleaning up the breakfast dishes. Her husband, Dick, had left an hour earlier for the funeral home where he worked.

On the other end of the phone, Louise was sitting at the table finishing her coffee. She wished she hadn't taken the call. This conversation was not how she wanted to start her day.

"I just think it's bad business for a church to sell a cookbook that starts out with party cake." Beatrice swished the dishrag around the skillet. She and Dick had eggs for breakfast. "You remember how much trouble we got into because of Lucy Seal's pears in port recipe in the first cookbook, don't you?"

"Verna Bean's holiday party cake doesn't have any alcohol in it, Bea. It has sour milk and butterscotch morsels."

"Butterscotch," Bea noted, rinsing out the skillet and placing it in the dish drain. "You think that doesn't draw up images for some people."

"You are being crazy, Beatrice. I don't understand why this bothers you."

"Someone will want to give us an eggnog cake recipe. You just wait."

"Is there an eggnog cake?" Louise asked. She poured herself another cup of coffee and then realized she had put the milk back in the fridge. She hated drinking her coffee black. She noticed the leftover milk in her cereal bowl. She shrugged her shoulders, set the phone down, poured the milk in her cup, and picked the receiver back up and placed it next to her ear. Beatrice was still ranting. "What's wrong with eggnog?" she asked.

"What's wrong with eggnog?" Beatrice repeated, sounding shocked that Louise would ask such a ridiculous question. "Do you remember the time Darlene brought eggnog to the church Christmas party?"

Louise snorted. "I certainly do," she replied, taking a sip of the coffee. She put down her mug and picked a cornflake from her tongue. "I also remember it being the most interesting Christmas pageant we've ever had."

She smiled recalling the event. Charlotte Stewart had been the pastor then and she had finished off a couple of refills of the drink before she knew what it was.

It was the first time Louise had ever seen the young woman actually slap her legs laughing. It was a lovely memory. Charlotte was usually a little uptight. All the cookbook committee members talked about it later. Even Margaret and Jessie, the two committee members who always challenged Beatrice and Louise when they gossiped about others, had noticed and enjoyed the pastor's behavior.

"The shepherds singing 'Grandma Got Run Over by a Reindeer' was not interesting. It was embarrassing," Beatrice said, recalling the pageant.

"Ah, it wasn't that bad. It was better than the wise men trying to break-dance for the Baby Jesus." Louise grinned. "Besides," she added as she took another sip from her coffee cup, "I think there may have been a little something else passed around the manger that year. It was really cold outside for the actors. I'm not sure that Joseph didn't have something extra stashed in the haystack."

"Who was Joseph that year?" Beatrice asked.

"I think it was Grady Marks," Louise noted. "He did it for a lot of years before he and Twila started going to Florida for the holidays."

"Uh-huh," Beatrice responded. "That's exactly what I'm talking about."

"What?" Louise said. "What are you talking about?"

"Grady told Darlene to bring the eggnog. He was the one who didn't see anything wrong with a spiked drink at a church gathering."

"Okay. But what does that have to do with having a recipe for a party cake in the cookbook?" Louise asked. She often had a difficult time following Beatrice in a conversation.

"Once Grady knew that Darlene's eggnog was being served for refreshments, he brought hard liquor into the nativity scene."

"Huh?" Louise asked, sounding very confused.

"I'm just saying one thing leads to another. First it's a party cake served at the women's fellowship.

Then it's bourbon balls at Easter. And then it's hard liquor being served to wise men and shepherds."

"Okay, so we won't put an eggnog cake recipe in the book. There's nothing wrong with Verna's cake, is there?" Louise wanted to know.

"Starting with the party cake just feels too liberal to me. Before you know it we'll be as loose as the Episcopalians. And we all know how much they like to drink."

"What kind of trouble did you get into because of the pears in port recipe?" Louise suddenly recalled something Beatrice had said earlier in the conversation. She hadn't remembered there being any problems stemming from the first cookbook.

"There was trouble is all I'm saying," Beatrice said.

"I don't recall any trouble."

"Well there was some," Beatrice responded. "There were calls and letters."

"Calls?" Louise was surprised at this new bit of information. She had not heard anything about this. "Who got calls?"

Beatrice cleared her throat. "I got a call," she said, sounding indignant.

Louise paused. She was trying to remember if she had ever heard this story before. Then suddenly she recalled the event. She sighed into the receiver.

"Bea, one phone call from Lettie Heck's mother

from the psychiatric center does not constitute trouble about a recipe."

"She made a valid point in the message she left on my answering machine," Bea replied. "And she wasn't in that place for very long. She had issues and she got help. I would think you of all people would appreciate her wisdom in seeking professional assistance."

"She doesn't have issues, she's crazy," Louise snapped. "And she didn't even buy a cookbook. She stole Lettie's during choir rehearsal."

"It doesn't matter how she got a cookbook," Bea said.

"I think if you steal something, you don't really have grounds to complain about the product."

Beatrice made a huffing noise.

"Besides, if I recall correctly, she was also upset that your prune cake recipe called for condensed milk and she said it was supposed to be evaporated."

"My mother only used condensed milk. Evaporated milk is too runny for that recipe; and just because we didn't hear all of the complaints about Lucy's fruit smothered in wine doesn't mean they weren't out there."

"What about letters?" Louise asked.

"What?"

"You said that there were calls and letters," Louise reminded Beatrice. "What letters did we get?"

"I got letters," Beatrice replied, sounding smug.

"Letters from somebody mad about the port recipe?"

Louise noticed the hesitation from the other end of the phone. She thought she heard her friend washing dishes. She imagined her standing at the window at her sink, holding the phone with her shoulder. She knew Beatrice often called her friends while she washed her dishes. Louise had told her that was why her neck hurt all the time but Beatrice hadn't seemed to make the connection.

"Well, no, not exactly," Beatrice finally said. She dried her hands.

"Well, what then?"

"I heard from a number of men whom I think were bothered by that recipe."

Louise considered what Beatrice was saying. "You mean the inmates from the jail?" Louise asked. She knew that Beatrice had added some unsold cookbooks in the gift bags the churchwomen made for prison inmates.

The list of acceptable items sent from the prison chaplain had been very specific. There was supposed to be only toothpaste, toothbrushes, shampoo, deodorant, and white athletic socks.

Beatrice had added the cookbooks because she decided the men might want something to read. As a result, the older woman had gotten quite a lot of attention from the inmates who sent her letters to the church hoping she would visit them. Louise recalled that the chaplain and the new pastor at the church were not pleased at the correspondences that took place.

"Those men deserve a cookbook that doesn't cause them to stumble," Bea noted. "A party cake just sounds like trouble."

"It wasn't the recipes that caused them to stumble," Louise responded. "Your perfume-scented letters were what caused stumbling. I'd even call it an out-and-out fall."

"I just thought they needed some uplifting."

"Yeah, but I don't think the uplifting they got was what you had in mind writing them back all those times."

"I was just trying to be a good Christian," Bea said.

"By dipping your letters in Chanel No. 5?" Louise asked.

"Every man deserves a fantasy, even prison inmates," she replied.

"Right," Louise said. "But just because they found out you were seventy years old and then started a protest and asked you to quit writing doesn't mean they were mad about a recipe with wine in it."

"Fine," Beatrice said sharply. "Put the stupid party cake recipe in there first. Put Darlene's eggnog in there. Why not put a bartending guide in there too? Add a few tips on making martinis and how to smoke crack in a pipe." Her voice was raised.

"Beatrice, is something wrong with you?" Louise asked. "You haven't seemed right about this holiday cake idea since we voted to do it. That's not like you."

There was a pause in the conversation, and Louise wondered if her friend had hung up on her. "Bea?"

"I'm still here." She waited. She didn't know what to say. She had been feeling this way for some time and had just never talked about it to anyone. Finally she said what she had thought for months. "My heart just isn't in this project."

"What! It was your idea!" Louise responded, sounding flustered. "If you didn't want to do it, why did you even suggest it?"

Louise had been very clear about her ideas regarding another cookbook project. She had not wanted to do the first one. She definitely did not want to be involved in the second one. Beatrice had convinced her and the other women in the church that this one would be less complicated than the first. She had promised them that since they would just have cake recipes it would be easier. And she guaranteed that it would bring in a lot of money by having a contest for the grand prize–winning cake, the Hope Springs Community Christmas Cake. Just like everything Bea suggested and wanted the churchwomen to do, she had done a great job selling the idea.

"I thought it would distract us," Beatrice replied.

“From what?” Louise asked.

There wasn’t a reply right away. Beatrice seemed to be thinking about what she was saying. She hadn’t really considered what this cookbook had been about. She never usually considered her reasons for anything she did. She saw every idea as an inspiration, and Beatrice loved the idea of being a source of inspiration. She had a history of pushing inspiration on others.

Beatrice had been the one who had the idea for the first cookbook. She shaved her head and made Charlotte and Louise and Jessie do the same when she thought Margaret was going to have to have chemotherapy after the first diagnosis. She organized the going-away party for Charlotte when the pastor left to run the women’s shelter out west. Beatrice organized events and planned activities all with the intention of inspiring others to be friends or become a community or just be engaged in something.

Beatrice had often wished she could be more like Margaret, the no-nonsense member of the community, the one who didn’t need anybody to do anything, the one everybody else relied on for wisdom or direction. Beatrice had also wished she could be like Jessie, similar to Margaret in the clarity of her decision making and always concerned about the right things. neither Margaret nor Jessie ever troubled herself with things of no consequence. And Beatrice could never seem to sort through what was really important and what was not.

She was a busybody and she knew it as well as everyone else, and even though she sometimes wanted to be more like her friends, up until this holiday cookbook she hadn't really minded that role. But now she knew that she was losing ground. She was not as dedicated to her causes. She knew the inspiration was no longer there.

Beatrice shut her eyes. She hadn't planned on having this conversation, especially with Louise. She pulled the phone over to the counter and sat down on one of the barstools.

"What would this project distract us from?" Louise asked again.

"From things," Bea replied. She knew she wasn't being completely honest.

"What things?" Louise asked. Then it dawned on her. The truth became crystal clear. She put down her coffee cup and sat back in her chair.

"Margaret's cancer," Louise said, sounding surprised and disappointed.

"Yes," Bea answered, glad that Louise had said it. "Yes, it's true. At the time I thought it would brighten our spirits. Margaret loves Christmas and she loves cakes and I thought . . ."

"You thought working on a cake cookbook would keep Margaret from remembering that her cancer has come back? You thought trying to sort through a hundred menu cards would make her forget the doctor's prognosis? You thought making her edit recipes for prune desserts and fruitcakes would help her in preparing to have another surgery, take more treatments?"

There was a pause in the conversation. Beatrice was hurt by her friend's opinion of the situation. Originally she had suggested the idea about the holiday cookbook with only the best intentions. She had really thought it would brighten everyone's spirits. Like all her ideas, she thought it would be the inspiration everyone needed.

She felt just like the other cookbook committee members, she was devastated by what was happening to their friend; and she was only trying to help things. But Louise was right and she knew it. Once again, Beatrice had tried to fix things with a project. And now not even she felt like seeing the project completed. It was already late in the autumn season and they hadn't even settled on the prize for the winning recipe. They weren't even sure how to pick the best cake.

The women weren't sending in cake recipes and Beatrice couldn't find any restaurant to honor the prize-winning recipe. She had grand ideas in the beginning that the winning cake could be featured on some nice restaurant's menu during the month of December. So far, no one seemed interested. No one was returning phone calls. She couldn't find any business to donate a prize. Usually the one never to be discouraged, the one who could pester even saints, especially in a project she initiated, Beatrice was just not being effective. She was as indifferent and uninterested in this cookbook and contest as everyone else.

Beatrice understood why. Margaret was the center of the Hope Springs community, not just the church, but the entire community. She was the glue that held them all together. She remembered how Jessie had described their friend. "Margaret was the pulse, the heartbeat, the blood supply" for that little rural area. Once the word had gotten out that after five years the cancer had metastasized again, this time in her liver, everybody was affected.

Once they heard the news, everybody in the church, and especially the cookbook committee, Margaret's three best friends, Beatrice, Louise, and Jessie, struggled. They found themselves feeling everything from shock to denial to anger to just trying to make a deal with God. No one could accept that Margaret's cancer was back. Beatrice tried to think of projects. Louise was just mad all the time, and Jessie teared up at every meeting.

"Beatrice, I'm sorry," Louise said, realizing that she had hurt her friend's feelings. "I know you were just trying to help. And I think a cake cookbook and cook-off will be nice and we can use the money to help Margaret pay for some of her bills. It was a good idea, Bea."

"It's not a cook-off, it's a recipe contest. And no, it wasn't a good idea. It was a stupid idea." She started to cry. "We'll end up spending more money than we make. And besides, I can't find any prize for the winning recipe. I don't know how to judge cakes. There's no such thing as a Christmas cake. It was a stupid idea," she repeated. "I always have stupid ideas."

Louise was shocked. She had never, not in thirty years of friendship, ever heard Beatrice sound so low. She couldn't even think of how to respond. Beatrice saying her idea was stupid? Louise suddenly wondered if Beatrice could be suicidal. She considered calling Dick to run over from the funeral home to be with her. "I'll take care of it," Louise responded, surprising herself by taking control of the cookbook project. "Just find a prize for the winner. I'll do the rest."

Beatrice felt a tear roll down her cheek. She nodded, not even realizing that Louise couldn't see her response. She wiped her face on a napkin she found at her elbow.

"Okay?" Louise asked.

There was no reply except what sounded like a nose being blown.

"We don't have to put the party cake recipe as the opening recipe in the book if you don't want to," she added. "We don't even have to use it at all. Okay?" Louise asked again.

There was still nothing from the other end.

"Beatrice, are you nodding?"

"Yeah," she finally answered.

“I can’t see you, remember?” Louise asked, her voice softening.

“Right,” Beatrice said. “I forgot again.”

“It’s all right, Beatrice. It’s going to be all right,” she said, trying to convince herself as much as her friend.

“Okay,” Beatrice said quietly. “Thank you, Louise,” she added.

“Yeah, you owe me,” Louise replied.

And the two friends hung up their phones.

# Hot Milk Cake

❄❄❄

4 eggs
2 cups sugar
¼ teaspoon salt
2 teaspoons vanilla
1 stick butter
1 cup boiling milk
2 cups flour
2 teaspoons baking powder

Beat eggs until they are thick and have changed to a pale yellow. Beat in sugar and salt until completely mixed with eggs. Add vanilla. Melt butter in boiling milk. Stir into sugar and egg mixture. Sift flour and baking powder and beat in very quickly. Bake in 2 9-inch cake pans at 350 degrees for 30 to 35 minutes.

# Chapter Two

Louise sat staring at the phone for a few minutes before she got up from the kitchen table. This cookbook and contest was not at all what she wanted to be working on. She needed to be in her garden, trimming away the old summer growth. She needed to put down more mulch, prune the rosebushes, pull up some old kudzu vines that were dying on her back fence.

She had intended to buy some pine straw from the garden center, find a little fescue grass seed for the bald spots in the front yard, pick up a few bulbs and autumn flowers. She had planned to spend the whole week out in the yard, but now she was going to have to put together Beatrice's holiday cooking project. And Beatrice was right about one thing. If they expected the finished project to be out and a winner selected by Christmas, they needed to step up the process. She sighed and shook her head, thinking about everything she would have to do.

Louise recalled the first cookbook the church ladies had completed. She thought about all the arguments she had with Beatrice, how they fussed about what went where and whose recipe got to be first in a section. She thought about all the trouble there was but then how wonderful the cookbook actually turned out.

She remembered that even though in the beginning she was dead set against the project, she had actually gotten more from it than anyone. Jessie, Margaret, Beatrice, even the pastor, Charlotte, had bonded so tightly because of that silly project. They were now the sisters she'd never had.

Louise considered that time in her life when the cookbook was being put together. She felt her chest tighten as she thought about Roxie, her best friend forever, the woman she loved, moving in with her a few months before she died. She remembered how she felt those months, so happy to be taking care of Roxie and so very sad to know that she was dying.

The cookbook committee had been the only reason she had lived through that grief. Those women had meant everything to her during that horrible time. Jessie had been a rock. Margaret had never let her down. Charlotte was an attentive pastor, and even Beatrice had never let her face a day alone. They had cared for her, gone to Maryland to bring her home after the funeral when she was really messed up, cooked her food, called her on the phone, stayed by her side for months. They had pulled her through her sorrow even though most of the time she had been kicking and screaming about her loss.

And now Louise wondered whether Margaret was the one dying, wondered if another cookbook meant another death. She shuddered at the thought, the awful thought of it. And if that was the case, if Margaret was terminal, she didn't know how those women would ever manage.

"I'm not dead yet," Margaret had said when the women had gathered around her in the doctor's office. He had just given the news about the findings from the CAT scan she had a few days earlier. He had reported that there was cancer, that she would need more treatments. The words had hung above them like some dark cloud. Margaret had already come through a second mastectomy and chemotherapy. He knew how long she had been struggling with cancer. He had not seemed optimistic at all, and they were devastated at the news.

Jessie, Beatrice, and Louise had accompanied Margaret to the doctor's appointment, just as they had to most of the others. They had been with her from the beginning of this illness five years ago, and they had kept the promises they had made. They did not let her face the disease alone.

After all they had gone through together, after the second surgery and the treatments, they could not accept that the cancer had returned. None of the three friends wanted to believe that it was true. And when the doctor gave his report, Jessie and Beatrice and Louise took it harder than the patient.

"You hear what I said?" Margaret had asked. "I'm not dead yet," she repeated. And the three women had tried to mask their disappointment, smiling at her, patting one another on the back, pretending the news was nothing more than just a tiny setback in their plans.

Louise sat at the table looking out the window and suddenly didn't care anymore about the overgrown vines and the shabby-looking garden. She didn't care about the unkempt rose bushes and the pigweed that had crept into her flower beds. She didn't even notice the dandelions. She could only think of her friend Margaret and what it would mean to her, to the others, if Margaret died.

"Knock, knock."

Louise heard the sound at the back door. She smiled. She knew it was Jessie. She recognized the voice, the silly way she always stood at a door and said the sound instead of making it by rapping her fist against the frame.

"Hey you," Louise called out, moving away from the table. She pulled open the door. "What are you doing out this morning?" she asked.

"Just had a feeling," Jessie replied.

Louise moved aside so that Jessie could walk through the door. Her smile widened and she nodded. She loved how the friends seemed to know when one needed the other.

"You want some coffee?" she asked.

"No, had plenty of that. I would take a glass of water though," Jessie responded. "I parked over at the school and walked here."

Louise looked down the road. “That’s got to be two miles,” she noted.

“I know it. My feet know it. My lungs know it.” Jessie took in a deep breath. “I’m trying to be more healthy.”

“Well, I don’t think killing yourself is the way to go. Have a seat,” Louise said, nodding toward the table, and Jessie walked over and sat down next to where Louise had just been.

Louise took down a glass and put a few cubes of ice in it and then poured water from the faucet. She knew that Jessie didn’t mind well water like some folks in the community. Louise drank it too, but some of the women had gone to getting fancy bottled water delivered to them from town. It had apparently become the “in” thing to do.

“Here you go,” she said, handing Jessie the glass. She reached over and got her mug from the table. Once she saw the bits of cereal in the bottom of it, she walked over to the sink and poured out what was left. She went over to the refrigerator and got the milk and decided to start over with her coffee.

“You okay?” Jessie asked after taking a sip of water. “I woke up with one of my funny feelings. I checked with all the children, with Lana and the baby. Everybody said I was crazy. Then I called Margaret but she seemed fine this morning. So I thought it might be you who was in trouble.” Jessie had premonitions, and she usually thought they had to do with those who were closest to her. That's why when she felt like something was wrong she always checked first with her family—her husband, James; or her grandson, Wallace, and his wife, Lana, and their baby, since they lived the closest to her.

Louise smiled at her friend. She loved the connection, the bond they shared. "Nope, your radar was a bit off." She sat down. "It is a cookbook committee member though," she added.

Jessie thought for a moment. "Beatrice?" she asked. She looked concerned. She had not thought of Beatrice as being in trouble. Jessie knew that Beatrice was one woman who always seemed to be in control. She rarely worried about Beatrice. "What's happened with Bea?"

"Her heart isn't in the holiday cookbook and contest project," Louise replied.

Jessie looked surprised and concerned. "Is she sick? Something wrong with Dick?" she asked. Like Louise, she knew something was terribly wrong if Beatrice lost interest in her project.

"She told me it was a stupid idea, that she always had stupid ideas," Louise told her friend. She had taken her seat next to Jessie.

"Beatrice?" Jessie asked, still not believing what she was hearing. "Beatrice Newgarden Witherspoon? Are we talking about the same woman?"

"Short, a little on the chubby side, hair short and teased too high?"

"My Lord," Jessie said, shaking her head. "Well, does she need to go to the emergency room or should we just call Dick to have her committed?"

Louise smiled. She and Jessie had often given their friend a hard time because of her projects, her ideas to fix things. They teased her about it, but they also loved her for the way she handled adversity. It was like comic relief when they faced difficulties. The cookbooks, the night they all shaved their heads, the sudden appearances of prune cakes when she thought someone was too uptight—Beatrice had a project or "fix it" idea for every brand of trouble. And she never ever considered it a stupid thing. Even when it backfired or turned out to be unnecessary, like the head-shaving event when it was revealed that Margaret wouldn't have to have chemotherapy that time after all, Beatrice had always stood behind her ideas.

Jessie's response to what Beatrice had said about the holiday cookbook and recipe contest was exactly like Louise's reaction. Beatrice was obviously depressed.

"Well, what are we going to do?" Jessie asked. She dabbed her mouth with a napkin from the table.

"I told her I would handle it," Louise replied.

Jessie sat back in her chair so hard she almost turned it over. "What?" she asked. "Did I hear what I think I heard?"

Louise rolled her eyes. She knew her decision was difficult to believe and she knew Jessie was giving her a hard time. Everybody knew what Louise thought about Beatrice's projects, especially the cookbooks.

"You're taking care of it?" Jessie said again. She shook her head and drank a swallow of water. She placed her glass on the table and fanned herself with her napkin as if she was suddenly feeling faint.

"Oh, stop it," Louise snapped. "Who else is going to do it?" she asked. "You keep that great-grandbaby all the time, still go to work at the mill when they call you. The preacher's wife certainly doesn't get involved in church affairs. Twila is getting ready to go to Florida. Elizabeth Garner has cataract surgery next week. Everybody knows Dorothy West is just crazy. And Margaret—" Louise stopped.

Jessie turned away. There was a pause between the friends.

"Margaret is going to be fine," Jessie finally said.

Louise nodded. She didn't want to contradict Jessie, but she knew she had her doubts about Margaret's future. "Well, regardless," Louise added, "Margaret doesn't need to be bothered about a cookbook right now."

"Yes," Jessie responded.

There was another pause. Jessie took another swallow of water. She put down the glass and wiped her forehead.

"Did they set the time for the surgery next week?" Louise asked. She knew that Jessie had gone with Margaret for her preadmission appointment at the hospital. They were all waiting to know what time the outpatient procedure to put in a portacath was scheduled. Someone was supposed to call Margaret and let her know when to show up on the day of the surgery.

"She's scheduled for the first slot on Wednesday," Jessie replied.

Both women understood the surgery involved placing the device under Margaret's collarbone that would become the IV site for the chemotherapy drugs. She had received one previously but it had been removed more than a year ago.

"So, that means getting to the hospital at six A.M.?" Louise asked. She was thinking ahead of arrangements she would need to make for being with her friends in the waiting room.

Jessie nodded. "It's always best to be first," she noted.

"Yeah," Louise responded, although not very convincingly.

"She'll just be in for a few hours," Jessie added.

Both women recalled that she had done well with the last surgery. She was groggy afterward; but she had not gotten sick from the anesthesia. It had not been too terrible for her. The chemotherapy, however, had been quite terrible. Margaret had gotten an infection at one point and was hospitalized with that for about a week. Everybody knew that she was not looking forward to another round of chemotherapy.

"Are we all spending the night with her Tuesday?" Louise asked, knowing she would certainly stay with her friend. Jessie and Beatrice, however, had spouses, so Louise wasn't sure if they would be bunking with her and Margaret or not.

Jessie shrugged. "We didn't really get that far," she replied.

Louise nodded.

They both glanced around the room. It was as if neither of them knew what to say.

"How do you think she's really doing?" Louise finally asked.

Jessie shrugged again and shook her head. "She's not talking much to me," she noted. "You?"

Louise shook her head in reply. "We haven't talked about anything except the weather and when a good time to work on the church flower beds would be."

"I think she's just holding up for us," Jessie surmised.

Louise thought about that. "Maybe. We didn't take the news very well," she added, recalling how shocked they had all appeared when the doctor came in with the news.

Before he came in, Beatrice had even cracked a joke that maybe it was time for Margaret to consider getting breast implants and that maybe the doctor could recommend a good plastic surgeon. She remembered how they were all laughing when the doctor finally walked into the room. No one was ready for the bad news.

"I think Margaret's just trying to take this the way she takes everything," Jessie said.

"As it comes," Louise finished the sentence for her friend. They both were very familiar with how Margaret handled problems.

Margaret never intended to fix things. She didn't run from trouble but she didn't try to make it something it wasn't either. She was as levelheaded and as calm as any woman Louise or Jessie ever knew.

"Remember what Charlotte used to say?" Louise asked.

Jessie nodded, recalling the former pastor and how much she thought of her parishioner. "Yep, even before there were bracelets and bumper stickers with 'WWJD' on them," she said, referring to the popular phrase from a few years before, "Charlotte was saying when she got in a jam she asked herself, 'What would Margaret do?' "

Both women smiled. They knew Charlotte loved all the people she served as pastor. But some people complained that she was too close to the members of the cookbook committee. Some of the other women were jealous of their relationships.

And yet, even among the committee members, everyone knew that Charlotte respected Margaret the most.

All three of the other women, Louise, Jessie, and Beatrice, knew that the preacher and Margaret had a very special bond. It hadn't, however, ever bothered them. They all knew that Margaret was the bravest, most faithful of them all. The fact that the preacher recognized that and honored that didn't trouble them or make them jealous; it simply made them respect the young woman even more. Secretly, they all approved of the special friendship.

As if the two women were reading each other's thoughts, they glanced up at each other, and Jessie shook her head. Neither of them had contacted Charlotte to tell her about Margaret.

"Do you think Margaret has called her?" Louise asked.

"I don't know," Jessie replied. "I tried once," she added. "But when the answering machine at the women's shelter picked up, I just didn't know what to say. I hung up before I left a message."

Louise nodded. She hadn't even had the courage to go that far. None of the three women wanted to break the news to their former pastor. They knew that Charlotte would be very upset.

"Maybe we should just wait until after the surgery. Then we can let her know when the treatments start," Louise offered.

Jessie narrowed her eyes at her friend, and Louise understood what the face meant. Charlotte would need to be told.

"Well, I suppose since you took care of Beatrice and agreed to take care of this holiday project, I will make the call to our young Charlotte." Jessie rolled her eyes as if she couldn't believe what she was agreeing to do.

"I think that's just right," Louise replied cheerfully. "I'll get Hilda Brown's hot milk cake recipe; and you tell Charlotte that the woman she respects the most in the world has cancer in her liver, a second metastasis." She kicked Jessie's chair a bit. "That's fair, sounds easy enough."

Both women smiled. They understood that nothing about what lay ahead for them in the next weeks before the holidays this year was going to be easy.

# Italian Cream Cake

❄❄❄

1 stick margarine or butter
½ cup vegetable shortening
2 cups sugar
5 egg yolks
2 cups flour
1 teaspoon baking soda
1 cup buttermilk
1 bag of coconut (14 ounces)
1 teaspoon vanilla
1 cup chopped pecans
5 egg whites, stiffly beaten

Cream margarine and shortening. Add sugar and beat until mixture is smooth. Add yolks and beat well. Combine flour and baking soda and add the creamed mixture alternately with the buttermilk. Add coconut, vanilla, and pecans. Fold in the stiffly beaten egg whites. Pour batter into 3 greased and floured 9-inch pans and bake at 325 degrees for 25 minutes or until cake tests done.

[*continued*]

## ICING

1 8-ounce package of cream cheese
½ stick melted margarine
16 ounces powdered sugar
1 teaspoon vanilla
chopped pecans
4 maraschino cherries, chopped
coconut

Beat cream cheese and margarine until smooth. Stir in powdered sugar. Add vanilla and continue beating. Ice cooled layers, sprinkling top layer with pecans, cherries, and coconut.

# Chapter Three

Beatrice hung up the phone after her conversation with Louise and sat back down on the barstool. She rested her chin in her hand, then tilted her head to watch the birds at the bird feeder outside the kitchen window.

It was one of the things she loved most about her house. She always made sure that she had a window in front of the sink and a bird feeder just a few yards away so that while she cooked and did the dishes, she could watch the birds as they gathered nearby. It was the way she liked to think about being connected to the animal kingdom. All the mothers, the female of the species, gathering the food for the young ones, all of them trying to have enough for themselves to sustain the energy necessary to do all that was required of them.

For most of her adult life, Beatrice would catch glimpses of the world outside while she was in the midst of her kitchen work, her cleaning and peeling and baking and canning. She loved to watch the birds. It somehow kept her active, kept her engaged in the tasks at hand, kept her doing what had to be done.

She would study the tanagers and the flickers as they spilled the seeds all around them or carried them off to nests in trees close by, and wonder if they ever watched her and if they felt the same camaraderie through the window that she did. She wondered if they even stopped to see another female taking care of her brood.

Bea looked closely and noticed the same birds that had been there all season. She saw the little brown sparrows and the black and white chickadees, their small feathered bodies flitting about, the seeds flying from the small shelf. Beatrice was glad Dick had replenished the food earlier. She knew the squirrels had gotten most of it the day before, and she didn't feel like refilling the container.

When they had first married, Dick had tried to get his wife to move the feeder, get it away from being so close to the two trees it stood between, to deter the squirrels from jumping on it, but Beatrice wouldn't have it.

She liked the feeder right where it was, right outside the window at the sink. She didn't care if the squirrels did manage a quick jump from the trunks of the big maples to the tall white pole where they easily shimmied up to the feeder. It didn't bother her that they could get to the food so easily. Besides, there were only a couple of squirrels left in the neighborhood anyway. The Bixbys from next door had gotten a new dog and he had run off most of the squirrels and rabbits. Lucky for Beatrice, he didn't seem to bother the birds.

She watched the morning action at the feeder and thought about the conversation she just had with Louise. She had surprised herself with the revelation she made about her heart not being in the holiday cookbook. She hadn't really known that she felt that way until she said the words out loud. Now that the fact was out there, that her heart wasn't in the project, she felt a bit relieved but also a little scared. She knew it wasn't like her to give up so quickly. She wondered if what Dick had said a couple of months ago was true, that she was depressed and needed to get some medication.

She recalled the conversation they had that led him to say that. He had been trying to get her to go out for dinner for weeks and she kept declining the offers. Beatrice used to love to go out to restaurants. She loved the movies and trade shows. But in recent weeks she only went out for church and various required meetings. She just didn't have the interest in leaving her house anymore.

When she had said to Dick that she didn't want to go out on a Friday night after he had purchased tickets to some country music show over in Siler City and had made dinner reservations at their favorite steak house off Highway 421, he had told her that he was concerned about her, that he had talked it over with his sister and his doctor, and that he thought Beatrice was clinically depressed and needed some help.

Beatrice had never thought of herself as the

depressed type. She knew several people from the community had claimed to be depressed. Her daughter's husband had even started taking some drug he had seen on the television because he said he felt the way the man on the commercial said he felt. And for the most part, Beatrice had tried to be sympathetic toward those facing that illness.

However, she had never admitted it because she liked to think of herself as being nonjudgmental and compassionate, but the truth was, she tended to look down on those people who battled with the mental illness of depression.

She was truly supportive of some folks who claimed to need medical or professional intervention because of intense sadness or fatigue, indifference, or other depressionlike symptoms. She understood why some people would be depressed.

She knew that Nadine Klenner needed help after her daughter was killed in that car wreck at the church. She didn't think that the young mother's condition was a pretense or a means of getting pity. She completely understood why Nadine needed to be in a psychiatric unit and take medications for some months after the accident.

She understood when her son-in-law sought assistance because he had just buried his father and was having to place his mother in a nursing facility. This was at the same time he lost his job and was diagnosed with the illness that had killed his father. Beatrice had encouraged him to get help.

It wasn't those folks who suffered tremendous losses or faced horrid tragedies that she judged for having problems with feelings of overwhelming sadness, or for saying they couldn't go to work anymore, or for admitting that they needed some additional help. There were lots of people that she believed should get professional assistance.

It was the ones who didn't seem to have anything wrong in their lives that made Beatrice raise an eyebrow when they said they were "under a doctor's care" for their depression. It was the ones in whom she didn't see anything that she would describe as "traumatic" or reasonable cause for a mental breakdown.

She just didn't understand how a healthy person who had a good job and whose family was intact, and who had a home and a car and good health could suddenly just feel indifferent about life, not want to get out of bed, or weep uncontrollably. She couldn't accept that a person couldn't shake the bad mood or the loneliness. She figured a person could pull herself or himself out of the pit of self-pity.

She had always thought a good prune cake could undo the knots or just getting outside would lift a person's spirits. She knew working in the garden and having a knitting project always made her feel better. And Beatrice understood that she had always managed the hardships of life, significant losses of a spouse, of siblings, and of her parents, disappointments in relationships, isolation, loneliness; she just didn't understand why everyone else couldn't either.

She thought about the former pastor of the church, Charlotte. She recalled how the young woman often seemed inattentive, somewhere other than where she was. Margaret had mentioned that she was concerned about her, that maybe she needed to talk to someone.

Beatrice, however, simply thought she needed to get out more, date some, leave the church on her day off. For three or more years, Beatrice had given her pastor craft books, flyers about singles meetings, flower bulbs for the beds around the house, books to read, anything to draw the young woman out of her sadness.

When she heard that the pastor was seeing a therapist, Beatrice thought Charlotte had gone to the dark side. She figured the pastor just wasn't praying enough, wasn't faithful enough; and she had questioned whether she should even have been in the ministry. Beatrice just didn't understand how a preacher—a person trained in seminary, one who knew all the scriptures, was supposed to help others, and was supposedly called to serve God—could feel withdrawn from her community, could wrestle with depression.

She pretended to understand, acted like she was

sympathetic with Charlotte and some of the others she had heard about who were going into therapy or having to take antidepressant medication, but the truth was, she just didn't understand. She had assumed a person could take care of those "feelings" herself. She thought if a person stayed busy enough, engaged enough in her family or community or a project, there would be no time for depression. She had really believed that a good prune cake, a regular Bible class, and volunteer work could push sorrow aside.

Until now.

Now it was she who didn't want to get out of bed or change out of her pajamas. She rolled out only because Dick was so noisy and so persistent in the mornings, she couldn't stay in there. She had lost her appetite, had difficulty remembering details, cried a lot more than she should about small things, insignificant things, things that never used to worry her, and she didn't care about the Hope Springs Women's Guild Christmas Cake Contest and Cookbook.

She submitted the idea when Margaret started getting sick, and although most of the women rolled their eyes at her as they always did and tried to get her to change her mind, they had agreed to the project, but only if she did most of the work. That had been weeks before and she hadn't done anything. She just didn't care whether the book was put together, or whether there was a Christmas cake for the community. She just didn't care about anything.

Her feelings of despair, she thought, did have to do with Margaret and the recurrence of the cancer; but Beatrice also knew that she had started feeling this way before they heard the news from the CAT scan. That information just seemed to make her worse, and now, she realized, it prevented her from being more proactive about her own condition.

Once Dick found out from Bea about Margaret's prognosis, he had left his wife alone these last couple of mornings when she wanted to stay in bed or didn't want dessert after dinner. He figured her sadness was appropriate after hearing the bad news about her best friend. He hadn't mentioned her going to the doctor again. But Beatrice didn't know how long Dick's empathy would last, and she didn't know whether she wanted to use Margaret's illness to justify or explain the way she had been feeling. In spite of that, however, she didn't know what to do.

She continued to watch the birds out the window. She noticed how the small ones had cleared away now that a blue jay was there. The long, slender bird pushed the others aside and perched right along the edge of the feeder. He seemed to enjoy his dominant posture, his high place in the bird kingdom. He ate a few seeds and appeared to dare the other birds to return.

Beatrice picked up the phone at her side and

dialed the funeral home. Betty Mills, the receptionist, answered.

"Betty, it's Bea. Is Dick around?" she asked, twirling the cord with her right hand.

"Hello, Beatrice," Betty said with her smooth funeral home voice. "How are you today?"

"I'm fine," Bea replied. "How are you?" she added, trying to be cordial. The truth was, she never really liked Betty. Bea thought she always sounded a little too sweet. Bea thought she talked down to the bereaved, treated them like children.

"I'm doing really well, hon," she responded. She cleared her throat. "I heard about your Christmas cake contest at the church. I think I'd like to enter my Italian cream cake," she said.

"That's nice, Betty." Beatrice thought an Italian cream cake didn't sound very Christmas-like, but she didn't really feel like discussing it.

"It was my grandmother's," Betty continued. "We had it every Christmas."

"That's real nice." Beatrice tried to sound interested.

"One year, there was a shortage on the maraschino cherries and Grandmother had to ride three hours over to Virginia to get a can." Betty sighed. "We loved that cake."

"That's special," Beatrice noted.

"So, what's the prize?" Betty asked.

"Um, we're still working on that," Beatrice replied.

"You know, our church gave one hundred dollars

for a winning recipe one time," Betty announced. "Lilly Clover won for some bean casserole."

"Okay." Beatrice was getting tired of the conversation.

"I guess your little church can't afford that though. But still, it would be nice to win," Betty said. "I'd like Grandma's cake to be honored."

"Is Dick there?" Beatrice asked. She was tired of talking to Betty.

"Oh, yes he is," the receptionist answered. "Let me get him for you." Then she paused. "I could just give him the recipe card, couldn't I?"

"Yep, that would be grand," Beatrice answered.

There was a pause from the receptionist, and Beatrice heard the bell on the front door ring. She knew someone was coming into the funeral home.

"Let me get Mr. Witherspoon for you," Betty noted quickly and put the call on hold before Beatrice could say anything else.

A few seconds passed and Dick picked up.

"Hey doll, what's up?" he asked.

"Why did you tell Betty about the cake contest?" she asked before giving any greeting.

"I don't recall telling Betty about your contest," he replied.

"Well, somehow she knew about it and you seem to like to talk to her about everything."

Dick sighed. "I didn't tell Betty about the contest and I don't like to talk to her about everything."

Beatrice wanted to cry but she didn't.

"Well, don't tell her anything else," she ordered. "Betty likes to make fun of our church because her pastor has a doctorate and they have a special choir with those shiny handbells and she thinks they're better than everybody else."

"Okay," Dick said softly, "I won't ever tell her anything about what's going on at church." He waited. "What did you call for?" he asked.

Beatrice could tell he was trying not to be mad at her. They had lots of these kinds of discourses lately. He had never argued with her but she had noticed that he seemed to be losing patience with her. He had even started staying longer at work than he used to. Beatrice now suddenly realized that he was avoiding her, avoiding coming home.

"Are you having an affair with Betty?" she asked, startling herself with the question.

Dick chuckled. "Is that why you called?" he asked.

"Are you evading the question?" Beatrice asked. Now she was starting to think it was possible. Maybe her husband was cheating on her, and she wondered if that was cause to be depressed.

"Bea, I am not cheating on you. I am not having an affair with Betty. You know she's married to my first cousin."

Beatrice considered that and realized she was talking crazy.

"Okay, you're not having an affair with Betty," she noted. "I believe you," she added.

"Great," Dick responded. "Now, is something wrong this morning? Do you need anything?"

She shook her head and then remembered the last part of her conversation with Louise. "No," she answered him. "I just wanted to see if you were coming home for lunch."

"No, dear," Dick responded. "I've got the Mackey funeral this afternoon. The family is coming at twelve-thirty." He paused. "I told you that at breakfast," he added.

"Oh, that's right, I remember now," although she didn't. "Did Edith take Fred's glass eye?"

"I don't think so, sweetie. What would she do with her dead husband's glass eye?" he asked.

"Make a necklace? I don't know. I just thought you gave people those kind of artificial parts."

"No," Dick said slowly. "Not here," he added. "Maybe some places do."

"Yeah, maybe," she responded. "So, see you at dinner then?"

"No, Bea, I've got Rotary tonight."

Beatrice then recalled the conversation they had earlier in the day. She had forgotten everything he had said after she talked to Louise.

"Oh, of course, I know that," she said, trying to sound like she had just made a minor slip-up.

"Have you talked to Margaret today?" he asked.

"No, why?"

"You just sound . . ." He paused. "I don't know, a little down," he added.

"I talked to Lou. She's taking over the cake project," she said.

"Louise?" he asked, sounding very surprised at that announcement. He knew Louise as well as anyone. She was not the cookbook chairperson kind of woman.

"Yes," Beatrice replied. "She's going to handle the remaining tasks except for finding a prize for the winner. I still have to do that."

Dick seemed to be thinking about this bit of news. "You're letting Louise take over?" he asked.

"Yes, well, I think she could do a little more this time anyway," Beatrice noted.

"Okay," Dick said, sounding unconvinced. "What are you doing the rest of the day?" he asked, knowing that the cookbook project had been the only thing she had been involved in during the past few months.

"I don't know," she said. "I'm sure there are things I will find to do," she added. "I'll think of something."

"Okay." He sounded hesitant to hang up the phone. "You call me if you need me," he instructed. "I'll have my cell phone."

"Right," Beatrice said. "I'll see you tonight."

She hung up the phone without even saying good-bye, and she watched as the blue jay flew away.

# *Holiday Pound Cake*

❄❄❄

2 sticks butter
½ cup shortening
3 cups sugar
6 eggs
3 cups flour
½ teaspoon baking powder
1 cup milk
1 teaspoon vanilla
2 teaspoons orange extract
1 tablespoon grated orange rind
½ cup nuts
½ cup raisins

Cream together butter, shortening, and sugar. Add eggs one at a time, beating thoroughly after each addition. Add one third of flour and baking powder and one third of milk, beating well after each addition. Repeat until all is used. Stir in flavorings, orange rind, nuts, and raisins. Pour into tube pan that has been well greased and floured. Put into cold oven. Then turn on oven and bake at 350 degrees for 1 hour and 15 minutes.

# Chapter Four

"Here it is," Margaret announced to no one except herself. "Holiday pound cake," she added. Then she glanced around and realized that she was talking to herself. She shook her head, glad that no one else had seen her. She didn't want anyone to think she had started chemotherapy treatments and lost her mind in the same week.

She had been searching for the old recipe ever since Beatrice mentioned the idea of a holiday cake cookbook to the Women's Guild. She wasn't really interested in the project, thought it was sort of lame, but she knew that once again Beatrice was simply trying to make things better for her and the other women in the community, and besides, truthfully, she was glad to have something else to think about except the test results and the upcoming surgery.

That was all she seemed to think about these last few days. She wondered if she would be sick from the treatments again. She wondered if she should hire someone to stay with her for a while after the surgery. She thought about prescriptions and insurance and what nightgown to take to the hospital and whether the cancer had already metastasized somewhere else in her body.

Unlike her friends, Margaret knew the cancer had recurred before there was a test. She knew it even before she started feeling sick to her stomach. Of course, she was hypervigilant, like most cancer survivors. She had been analyzing herself every day. And she just had a sense after the last surgery, and even with an "all clear" prognosis, that the cancer wasn't finished with her, that there was more to this event than just the lumps in her breasts and the one round of treatments.

She couldn't explain it, never talked about her premonitions to anyone. She knew if she did, her friends would just say she was anxious, that everybody felt as she did after a cancer diagnosis, and maybe that was true. Maybe because of her anxiety and worry, she had even talked herself right into liver cancer; she didn't know. She just knew that what lay ahead was not anything she wished for herself. She certainly did not want cancer. She preferred to be finished. She did not want to spend any more time at the hospital, and she did not want to face the treatments that she knew were once again inevitable.

Margaret placed the recipe card on the table, put up her recipe box, and went to the bedroom. She stood in front of the mirror on her dresser and lifted her blouse and looked at her flat, scarred chest again. She must have done that a hundred times a day, but she just needed to keep looking at it, as if seeing what had been taken from her gave her strength, helped her accept the disease inside her body.

She held her blouse up and studied herself. She noticed the right side, the scar that used to be a breast. Then she looked at the left side, the newer scar slightly more raised than the other.

She could see how her chest appeared merely flat and smooth, like her back or down along her sides under her arms. She looked closely at herself and realized that it wasn't that upsetting. She was too old, she told herself, to worry about not having breasts. She had been asked about reconstruction surgery. She knew that many women who had breast cancer had chosen that option. She knew lots of women who added implants, but she had decided the first time that was of no interest to her. And now, studying herself as she was, she knew she had made the right decision.

She had only herself to please, and she was just as pleased to be without breasts as she was to have a doctor build her a set. Now she was without both of them, and at least, she thought, she was even. Both sides of her matched, and in some way, that actually felt more normal than she had when just one breast was taken and she felt misshapen and off balance.

She lowered her blouse and looked at her face, considered losing her hair, her eyebrows, wondered if she should go ahead and get a wig or just wear hats and turbans like some of the other women she had seen. She already had a couple of wool caps from the last time she faced chemotherapy. She knew they were sitting on a shelf in the closet.

She slid her fingers through her short hair and smiled as she remembered the night all her friends had shaved their heads after the first surgery. She thought about how panicked she was when they started, how she tried to make them stop; but then how it felt to see their gift, their sacrifice, and how deeply and well she slept that night as she lay near her four baldheaded friends.

Then Margaret laughed when she remembered how it was when she didn't have to have chemo, how shocked the women were when they heard the news that she would keep her hair while they would have to be bald without her. Louise had chased Beatrice out of the doctor's office. Margaret had gotten a big kick out of that.

She recalled how the women, her friends, celebrated the success of that first surgery and how Charlotte, the former pastor, had told Margaret that she had prayed for that very result. Charlotte hadn't even minded that she had shaved her head for nothing, she had said.

Margaret stood staring at herself in her mirror and wished Charlotte was still in town. Hope Springs had gotten a new pastor almost three years ago, after more than a year of searching. Margaret liked the new fellow just fine. He was from the area, wanting to get back before he retired. So he was older and he was a good preacher, prayed gentle prayers; but he was a man, and try as he might, he could not be present with Margaret in this crisis in the way that young Charlotte had been able to be.

Margaret thought about the two pastors and didn't know if it was just because Charlotte was a woman and he was a man or if it was their personalities. Charlotte was often quiet, never pretended to know something she didn't. It was this kind of humble way for a minister to act that Margaret preferred to the new pastor's way, which was more of a "take control" attitude.

In the few times he had visited Margaret about one thing or another, it was as if the man couldn't sit with silence, needed to fill a room with words. And sometimes, even if they were lovely words, they seemed insincere, out of place. When she felt sad or worried or disconnected, Margaret preferred silence to words. But, she thought, as she left the bedroom and headed back into the kitchen, it didn't matter anyway. Charlotte was in New Mexico and her pastor was now Reverend Tom Joles. He talked too much but he was attentive to her. It was as it was, and there was nothing to do about it.

Margaret walked out of the bedroom and into the kitchen. She went to the refrigerator and pulled out the pitcher of tea. When she shut the door, she noticed the photograph that Charlotte had sent about two years ago. She slid it out from under the magnet and held it.

The photograph was of the young woman standing on top of a mountain. The sky was pink and red and orange, the sun dropping behind her. There weren't many trees, it was a barren landscape, but it was breathtakingly beautiful, and Margaret loved the picture. Charlotte's face was glowing, as if she had just hiked to the summit; and the older woman could never remember seeing her friend look so healthy and alive.

When they had spoken on the phone after Margaret received the photograph, she had kidded Charlotte that she must have fallen in love, she looked so happy. The young woman had simply said, "No, Margaret, it's just how it is out here. I know it sounds weird," Charlotte had added, "but I feel like myself here, like I can breathe here. It's like I've come to a place of perfect peace."

And in some way that she couldn't explain, Margaret had understood. She had recognized that expression from the photograph. She knew what her young friend meant. She knew what Charlotte was talking about because she had felt that way too, but only once.

It had been a very long time ago. She was just a child when she felt it and she grew up thinking that after that one time, she would never feel that way again, and she was right, she hadn't.

It had happened when she was ten, and it was just a few months before her mother died. The family had driven to her mother's home place,

Goodlett, Texas, just near the border of Oklahoma. They had all piled into the car and driven for hours just to get her mother home. Margaret didn't know at the time that her mother was dying; she only thought they were going to visit family, spend Christmas with her grandparents, with cousins and aunts and uncles she had never met.

The moment of perfect peace happened when they went to church late on Christmas Eve. It was cold and dark, and the church was decorated with candles and smelled of cedar and pine. The choir was singing and Margaret was sitting next to her mother, and she glanced around at her family all together, the warmth of it all, the loveliness of it, and she turned to look at her mother and her mother was glowing. Just like an angel, Margaret had thought. She had never seen her so beautiful. And Margaret remembered thinking that this was the finest, the best moment of her life. And for that one moment, it was.

The next day, after opening a few gifts and eating a big meal, the family left. Margaret and her siblings and her father got back in the car and drove home, leaving her mother with her family, "just to visit," she had told her youngest daughter. But Margaret learned later it was to die. Her mother had gone home to be cared for by her mother and her sisters, and she had died in her childhood home.

For the rest of her life, Margaret had never had a

moment of peace like that again. And she had never returned to Texas. Later in the final days of that winter season when her mother did die, all her brothers and sisters went back to Goodlett for the funeral, but Margaret had stayed with her cousin in North Carolina. Sometimes over the years her sisters and brothers would go to Goodlett, visit cousins, visit the grave; but not Margaret. For some reason she had never named, never considered, she never went back.

It was, she thought as she poured herself a glass of tea and sat down at the table, something she hadn't thought of in years. But somehow, seeing the photograph of Charlotte, that look of perfect peace, she remembered how she felt the Christmas of her tenth year and how she had never managed to feel that way again. She thought of Goodlett, Texas, and how she had never gone to say good-bye to her mother.

And now, she sighed deeply, it was too late to do anything about any of it. Cancer in her liver, chemotherapy, maybe radiation; she was old and she was sick. She had waited too long to see if she could find that kind of peace again, have that feeling again that she had when she was ten and sitting next to her mother. She had waited too long to sort through all the things she had felt about her mother and about her death.

"Miss Margaret, are you home?" the voice came from the back porch.

The kitchen door was opened and Margaret could see Lana Jenkins, Jessie's granddaughter-in-law, standing at the steps with her little girl, Hope, resting on her hip.

"Lana, hello, come in," Margaret said as she stood up from the table and opened the door.

The young mother and her child walked up the steps and headed into the house.

"Good gracious, but she's too big for you to carry."

"I know," Lana responded. "But she's not feeling well today so . . ." She looked down at her daughter.

"So, you carry her," Margaret finished the sentence.

"Right."

The little girl dropped her head on her mother's shoulder and closed her eyes.

"What's wrong with her?" Margaret asked, studying the little girl to try to figure out the problem.

"I think it's just a virus. She was sick during the night and then woke up with a little bit of fever." Lana smoothed the hair across her little girl's brow. She glanced back up at Margaret. "I tried to call Miss Jessie because Wallace is out of town, but I can't reach her and I've got to get to the school for a class this morning." She seemed a bit distraught. "I've got a test."

Margaret nodded. She knew that Lana was in

nursing school and that Hope was in kindergarten. She understood the predicament and already knew what the young mother was asking. Hope had stayed with Margaret lots of times.

"It's fine for her to stay here," she said, reaching out her arms to take the child.

Hope held out her arms and went to the older woman.

"I'm really sorry about this. I've called everybody I know and everybody's gone. I tried to call Miss Jessie's cell phone but she never turns the thing on. Mr. Jenkins is not answering the house phone. And my family is all out of town at my great-aunt's funeral. I just didn't know who else to ask. I feel like such a bad mother, leaving her with somebody else."

Margaret was shaking her head. "It's fine. I don't mind. And Lana, you are not a bad mother. You're a student and you need to finish your classes. You are doing a very responsible thing to leave her with a friend."

"I just didn't think I should send her to school with a fever," Lana added.

"You were right. And this is a perfect solution. I don't have anything planned for today, so I'm happy to stay with her."

Lana smiled, and Margaret nodded at her. She studied the young woman. She figured that Lana hadn't heard about her prognosis because if she had, Margaret knew Lana would never have asked for help. And actually Margaret was glad to be treated as if nothing was wrong. She liked how normal it felt to be asked to babysit her best friend's great-granddaughter.

"I only have to take this test and then I can come right back. It shouldn't be more than a couple of hours. I have some extra clothes for her in case something happens, and here's some juice and a couple of toys." She handed Margaret the bag.

Margaret took it from her and began waving her out the door. "Go, it's all right. Hope and I will be fine, won't we, sugar?" she asked.

Lana waited and then felt her daughter's brow again. "I think the fever is gone now. I gave her a couple of Tylenol and she feels cooler to me."

Margaret nodded. "I'm sure it's just that bug going around. I know a few of the other children from church were sick Sunday." Margaret had stopped by the nursery before the worship service to speak to one of the workers. She had commented how low the number of children was that morning. That was when she heard about the virus going around.

"Okay," Lana responded. "Thank you, Miss Margaret. I don't know what I'd do without you and Miss Jessie."

Margaret smiled. "Just make a good grade on your test and promise to take care of us all when we're sick, and that will be a plenty."

Lana smiled. "That's a promise." She squeezed

her daughter on the shoulder. "I'll be back real soon, sweetie," she said.

Hope nodded slowly and watched as her mother walked out the door and down the back steps. Margaret stood with her on her hip for a few minutes. She liked the feel of the child in her arms. She rocked her a bit from side to side as they heard the car pull away. She felt Hope's brow too and noticed that the little girl seemed a bit warm to the touch, but not too hot.

"Well, I think I have a couple of Popsicles in the freezer. Do you think you might like to have one of those?" she asked.

She felt the little girl nod her head against her neck.

"How about you sit here at the table and I'll get us a couple." She slid the little girl into a chair. "You like cherry or grape?" she asked.

"Cherry," the little girl replied, and placed her hands on the table.

Margaret walked over to the refrigerator and opened the small freezer door on top. She searched inside and found the box of Popsicles. She had bought the box over the weekend as she was preparing for the surgery and the treatments. She knew she would appreciate them when she was home from the hospital. She pulled a couple out and shut the door.

"Here's cherry," she announced to her guest and handed the Popsicle to her. She grabbed a napkin and wrapped it around the end. "I think I've got orange," she announced, sitting down beside Hope. She unwrapped hers and smiled at the orange treat.

"Nothing like a good Popsicle when your stomach hurts," she said.

The little girl nodded as she licked.

After they finished and had washed their hands, Margaret walked with Hope into the den and turned on the television. Hope picked a channel that was showing cartoons and sat on the floor. Margaret grabbed a pillow from the bedroom and a quilt from her linen closet. She made a nice place for Hope to lie and watch television and then walked back into the kitchen to clean up. She peeked in the room a few minutes later and noticed that the little girl was already asleep.

It wasn't long before she saw the car drive up and watched as Jessie hurried up the steps. Margaret met her at the door. She held her finger to her lips to let her friend know that Hope was sleeping close by. Jessie nodded.

"I'm so sorry," Jessie whispered. "I just turned on the phone," she added, walking in beside Margaret and then leaning so that she could see Hope asleep in her friend's living room.

"I hate that this happened," she said to Margaret.

"Why?" Margaret asked. "This is how we do things here, remember?"

"I know, but with everything going on for you, you don't need a sick child in your house," Jessie replied. She turned to her friend. "How long have you had her?" she asked.

"Oh, you just missed Lana. And it's fine. I've got an iron stomach, remember. I don't ever catch these little bugs. I just get cancer," she added, punching Jessie in the arm.

"Right," Jessie responded.

Margaret could see her friend's concern. "I'm fine," she said, trying to reassure Jessie.

"I know," Jessie replied. "You're going to be fine," she added.

"So, where have you been?" Margaret asked.

"With Louise," Jessie said. "I stopped by there after my walk." She leaned against the table. "Beatrice put her in charge of the holiday cookbook and contest."

"What?" Margaret was very surprised. "Is Beatrice sick?" she asked, wondering if her friends weren't telling her their own problems anymore, if they were protecting her from something.

"She's just acting different," Jessie said. "No, nothing's wrong as far as I know," she added.

Margaret shook her head. "And Louise, is she sick?" She smiled.

Jessie laughed. "I know, both of them are acting pretty strange."

"Well, I never thought I would see the day when Louise was handling a Women's Guild project that Beatrice started and then turned over to someone else." Margaret scratched her head in amazement.

"We live in different times," Jessie announced.

"That's for sure."

The two friends paused for a minute.

"Have you told Charlotte yet?" Jessie asked.

Margaret looked up at her friend. Then she turned back to notice the photograph on the refrigerator she had been studying earlier in the morning. She shook her head. "Not sure how to," she replied.

Jessie nodded. "You want me to call her?" she asked.

Margaret considered the offer and then glanced up at her friend. "Since you're here, why don't we both call her?" And she turned to the little desk in the corner of the kitchen where she kept her address book and Charlotte's phone number. "What time is it in New Mexico, anyway?" she asked.

# Hummingbird Cake

❄❄❄

3 cups sifted flour
1 teaspoon baking soda
1 teaspoon salt
2 cups sugar
1½ cups cooking oil
3 eggs
2 cups chopped bananas
1 cup crushed pineapple (include juice)
1 cup coconut
1 cup nuts
1½ teaspoons vanilla

Mix all the ingredients in a bowl and stir by hand. Pour into 3 greased 9-inch cake pans and bake at 350 degrees for 20 to 25 minutes.

## ICING

2 sticks soft margarine
1 8-ounce package of cream cheese
1 box powdered sugar (16 ounces)

Mix ingredients with mixer and spread between layers and on top.

# Chapter Five

When the call came in from North Carolina, Charlotte was trying to figure out how she was going to fit one more person in the shelter. She was already over the occupancy limit, but she knew she was going to have to find one more bit of space. She was not going to turn anyone away.

The hospital had called about a young woman earlier that morning. The social worker said that she had nowhere else to go and was recovering from the most recent and most dangerous attack from her boyfriend. She had a broken pelvis and two fractured ribs. She was young, not quite twenty, but she had no family nearby and nowhere else to go. She was over the age limit for foster care and the hospital wouldn't keep her any longer.

This victim, like so many of the others Charlotte served, had fallen through the cracks in the broken system that tried to assist battered women. Charlotte knew that if she didn't find this woman a bed and a place in the shelter, she would end up back with her abuser. Charlotte had seen it happen too many times.

"I found the cot," Maria was yelling from the closet that was down the hall from the office. "I hope she's a really small person," she added.

Charlotte assumed she was referring to the condition of the cot and that it couldn't hold a lot of weight. Recalling what the furniture was like for most of the shelter, she knew it was probably not in great shape.

She got up from her desk and headed in the direction of the volunteer who was trying to help her set up a space for the new client. Immediately she saw what Maria had meant. The legs on the cot were bent and wouldn't be able to hold a child, much less an adult.

"That's the only one left?" she asked, glancing behind the woman and looking into the closet.

Maria nodded. "The other three are in the back bedroom. Loretta's children are using them."

Charlotte sighed, remembering Loretta had been in the shelter for only a couple of weeks and her children were too big to share cots and too small to send to another facility. She had faced situations like this numerous times since she had taken the job as executive director of the battered women's shelter in Gallup, New Mexico. She had been there for only a couple of years, but she had learned a lot, including how to make room for twenty people in a house that was supposed to hold only ten.

"Let me see if I can fix it," she said.

Maria handed the bent cot frame to Charlotte, who stretched it out and placed it in the hallway. She tried to straighten the bottom legs, pushed and pulled, thinking she could snap it back in place, and then she just gave up. "How about the air mattress? We still got that?" she asked.

Maria nodded. "It's in the garage," she replied. "I'll go get it."

Charlotte tried to fold the cot back up but after her handiwork, it was completely broken. She pulled it down the hall, out the front door, and placed it on the porch. The next day was trash day, and she would place the broken bed next to the garbage cans when she left that afternoon.

She stood for a moment at the door, trying to see if Maria needed any help finding the mattress. She was planning to go out to the garage when she heard the phone ring. She considered not answering it for fear that it would be another request for space. Finally she walked over and picked up the receiver.

"Charlotte speaking," she answered.

"Jessie and Margaret calling," Margaret said. Her voice sounded cheerful.

"Hey!" Charlotte responded. She quickly moved around her desk and sat down. She was always glad to hear from her friends from North Carolina. "What's going on with you two?" she asked.

"We were just thinking about our favorite woman preacher and decided to check on whether or not she was done with her life searching and wanted to come back home." Margaret wanted the conversation to be as uplifting as possible.

"Hello, Charlotte." Jessie had taken the phone to greet her as well.

"Hey Jessie," the young woman responded. "Well, this is a lovely surprise." Charlotte could feel her smile widen. "Ya'll having a cookbook committee meeting?" she asked.

The two women laughed. They knew Charlotte didn't know about Beatrice's latest project.

"Funny you should mention that," Margaret responded. "We were calling to get a recipe."

"Are you serious?" Charlotte asked. "I was just kidding."

"I know you were, but you know how we love to put cookbooks together down here."

"Really?"

"Cakes actually," Margaret explained. "This one is just for cakes."

"Cakes," Charlotte repeated.

"That's right. So, what's your favorite cake recipe?" Margaret asked, sounding very professional.

"Cake?" Charlotte asked again. "Well, I guess that would have to be hummingbird cake."

"Hummingbird cake?" Margaret asked. "What is a hummingbird cake?"

"It has pineapple and coconut in it. Real fresh-tasting. One of the women here at the shelter makes it," she added. "But are you really looking for cake recipes?" she asked.

"Hmmm . . . hummingbird cake. Sounds

interesting. You ever heard of hummingbird cake?" Margaret lowered the phone and asked Jessie.

Jessie considered the question and then shook her head. "What has it got in it?" she asked.

"Coconut, pineapple," Margaret replied, raising the phone again. "What else is in it, Charlotte?"

"Bananas and nuts. It has a cream cheese icing," Charlotte said. "But you didn't answer me, are you really putting together another book?" she asked.

"It's the truth. Beatrice is doing another cookbook for the church. A cake cookbook," Margaret replied.

"Beatrice doing another cookbook?" Charlotte repeated, laughing. "Why is she doing that? Is something wrong at the church?"

Margaret slid the receiver down past her chin. "She wants to know if something is wrong at the church," Margaret noted to Jessie.

Jessie smiled. She knew Charlotte was just teasing about Beatrice but she didn't realize how close to the truth she was. She lifted her eyebrows in Margaret's direction. "Do you want me to leave?" she mouthed the words to Margaret.

Margaret shook her head and held out her hand for Jessie to hold.

"Margaret, you still there?" Charlotte asked. "Is something wrong with the Women's Guild?"

"Actually, Charlotte, something is wrong with me," she finally responded.

There was silence on both ends of the conversation. Charlotte waited for more from her friend. She was stunned by the answer.

"The cancer is back," Margaret added.

Charlotte didn't know what to say. The news hit her hard. She leaned back in her chair and swiveled around to look out the window. She saw two of the clients outside pulling weeds from around the fence.

"Where?" she finally asked.

"In my liver," Margaret replied. "I start treatments in a couple of weeks."

Jessie turned away. She could feel the tears gathering in the corners of her eyes. She knew how hard this conversation was for Margaret.

"When did you find out?" Charlotte wanted to know. She could feel the sudden shallowness of her breathing.

"A couple of weeks ago. I hate having to tell you over the phone," Margaret said. "I didn't know how to tell you."

Charlotte closed her eyes. She knew the possibility of recurrence in cancer patients was always there; she had just never allowed herself to think about that with her good friend Margaret. Ever since they had gotten the good news about the first surgery and about the lack of necessity for further treatments, she had only had positive thoughts about Margaret and her prognosis. Once the cancer came back in her other breast, she considered it a bad sign; but Charlotte thought they would eradicate it completely with the chemotherapy and radiation.

"Are you doing the chemo by IV?"

"Yes," Margaret replied. "I'll have the portacath put in next week," she added. "We won't know for sure when the treatments start until after that."

"Everybody going with you?" Charlotte asked, referring to the three friends from the cookbook committee.

"They won't have it any other way," she replied.

"Oh, Margaret." The tears started to fall. "I'm so sorry," Charlotte said. "I wish I were there. I wish I could be with you too."

"I know," Margaret replied. "That's part of the reason I didn't want to tell you. I didn't want you to feel like you needed to come." She shook her head remembering how Charlotte had come back for the second surgery and stayed with her for more than a week. "I'll be fine."

Charlotte waved at the two women outside when she saw that they were waving at her. It was Sophia and Victoria, two younger women who had been in the shelter for a number of months. They had arrived about the same time and had become great friends to each other.

"I could see if I can get someone to cover for me." Charlotte was trying to figure out if she could take off a few days and go back to be with her friend.

"No, no," Margaret said sharply. "There's no reason for you to come. This is a simple surgery. I won't be in the hospital overnight. I don't want you to come. It's too much."

Charlotte knew it was impossible to think about taking days off any time soon. She was understaffed as it was, and now that they were beyond the occupancy rate, she was going to have to figure out how to help some of the women transition out of the shelter and into permanent housing. None of the volunteers was capable of that.

She knew it was the worst possible time for her to think about leaving the shelter. It was getting to be the holidays, and she knew they were difficult times for the women. Some of them would want to go back home and try to make it work with their abusive husbands. Everyone needed extra support during the last months of the year. Charlotte knew she couldn't get away.

"I'm so sorry," Charlotte said, the only thing she could think to say.

"I know, me too," Margaret replied.

"Well, how are you doing with this?" Charlotte asked.

Margaret took a few moments before answering. She smiled at Jessie, and Jessie seemed to understand that Margaret needed privacy. Jessie got up from the table and went into the den to be with Hope.

"I'm okay," she responded, but she knew she didn't sound very believable. "Well, I mean, I'm trying to be okay."

"Are you scared?" Charlotte asked.

"A little," Margaret replied. "I dread the treatments and all the hospital stuff, all that probing and pricking." She paused. "Of course, maybe some women would like that part." She was trying to add some humor to the somber conversation.

"That's true," Charlotte responded. "I've got a few women staying here who would love a little probing and pricking, especially the pricking." She smiled.

Margaret was surprised at her young friend. She could tell a lot had changed for Charlotte since taking a job out of a church. She seemed much looser.

"Seriously," Charlotte noted, "you okay, really?"

Margaret took in a breath. "I'm okay," she said. "And I'll be fine. I'll make sure they call you when the surgery is over."

"What day is it again?" she asked.

"It's Wednesday, first thing," Margaret noted.

"Okay," Charlotte responded. "But I want us to talk more, at least twice a week from now on."

Margaret smiled. "Of course. I would like that very much."

There was another pause in the conversation. Charlotte wanted to ask her friend what she thought about the prognosis, how she felt about it, whether she thought of death; but it was all too much. She didn't know how to ask such questions.

"So, what's this cookbook thing that Beatrice has got going?" It was the best that she could do.

"Holiday cake cookbook," Margaret replied, sounding relieved that the hardest part of the conversation was over. "She thought it would be a good idea to have a contest to name the Hope Springs Christmas Cake and then do a cookbook with all of the recipes included."

"Well, it sounds like a lovely idea. Are you in charge of editing all of the recipes?" Charlotte asked. "Or are you the judge for the best cake?"

"Neither. I'm just gathering a few cards and handing them over," Margaret responded.

Charlotte smiled. She knew Margaret didn't mind the project and she also knew that Margaret was doing more than what she was saying to make the cookbook and the contest a success. Margaret was a very supportive and loyal friend, especially to Beatrice.

"You want me to send you the hummingbird cake recipe?"

"I think that would be nice," Margaret replied.

"You think I might win?" Charlotte asked. "Or do you have to live in Hope Springs to have the winning recipe?"

"I don't know the rules," Margaret said. "But I think that since you once lived in Hope Springs and have served as the pastor of the church, you have as much right to enter a cake recipe and be the winner as anybody else."

"Then I'll mail that recipe card to you right away."

"I'll let Beatrice know," Margaret announced. "She'll be glad to know you've taken up baking."

"I bet she will be."

The two women hesitated.

"Tell Jessie I said hello and that I love her," Charlotte said. "And Margaret"—she turned back around and leaned her elbows on the desk—"I love you too."

"I love you, Charlotte. And everything is going to be fine," Margaret said.

"I know," Charlotte responded. "And I'm the one who is supposed to be saying that to you."

Margaret smiled. "I'll talk to you next week."

"Tuesday evening," Charlotte said.

And the two women hung up their phones.

# Section Two

❄❄❄

# Ambrosia Cake

❄❄❄

2 cups sour cream
2 cups white sugar
1 12-ounce package of frozen coconut
1½ cups Cool Whip
3 oranges, peeled and chopped
1 box Duncan Hines butter or yellow cake mix
orange juice

Combine sour cream, sugar, and coconut and let set overnight. Blend 1 cup of the mixture with Cool Whip. To the remainder of the sour cream mixture add oranges. Prepare cake mix according to package directions in 2 9-inch pans, orange juice instead of water. Cut 2 layers into 4 layers. Put the sour cream mixture between layers. Frost cake with Cool Whip mixture. Keep in refrigerator at least overnight.

# Chapter Six

"I think you should just tell the hospital to keep this girl another day. We've got no room for her here. And with the injuries they said that she has, you can't take care of her here. You try to do too much, Charlotte."

Charlotte knew that part of what Maria was saying was true. She wasn't able to take care of someone who had a lot of physical needs, but she was not about to turn someone away, especially a young girl being released from the hospital. "We will make room for her, Maria. Just put the mattress in the front bedroom. There's space next to the closet. We'll figure this out. Everything will be fine."

Maria sighed and walked down the hall to do what was asked, and Charlotte sat at her desk thinking about the phone call she had just had with Margaret. She just couldn't think about the new client; she was still too upset about her friend.

She knew that the recurrence of cancer, and in the liver, was a terrible report. She recalled from her time as a pastor and visiting so many sick people in the hospital that liver metastasis was never a good sign of things to come. There wasn't usually any surgery performed to remove the cancerous part. It was usually a sign that cancer was winning in a body and there was nothing more that could be done.

The fact that Margaret was having treatments meant that the doctor hadn't given up on her, and Charlotte knew that sometimes chemotherapy could wipe out the disease or at least add a few years to a person's life.

She tried to think hopeful thoughts, tried to imagine that this was nothing more than just a little setback for Margaret, but she could not push from her mind the idea that Margaret, her dear sweet friend Margaret, was dying.

She thought about the others, about Louise and Jessie and Beatrice, and wondered how they would handle the situation, how they were handling it even now. She knew they would have a very difficult time if Margaret died soon. None of them would be able to face such a death. Margaret was everything to them.

She considered the cookbook scheme of Beatrice's and wondered if that was helping things even a little. Charlotte smiled when she recalled the last cookbook, all the meetings, all the conversations about the recipes and what should and shouldn't go into the book. She knew the church had lost money on the project, that there were still cookbooks sitting in the storage room at the church; but she also knew that it had been a good idea and that it had completed what Beatrice had set out to do. The project had brought them closer. It had helped make the women, the entire church, more of a community than it had ever been. She assumed that was the reason that no one had complained about the lost income. The church members were glad for what had come from the project.

She jotted herself a note to get the recipe for the cake she had told Margaret about and then looked at her calendar, trying to see if there was any time that she could get back to North Carolina before the end of the year. Every day was filled with meetings and court appearances and fund-raisers; she didn't see how she would be able to leave any time soon.

Charlotte shook aside the thoughts of Margaret and a full calendar when she heard the car in the driveway. A few minutes passed and then there was a knock at the door. When she got up from her desk and walked toward the entryway, she saw first a figure shadowed by the sun, then the face of the newest resident of St. Mary's House.

"Is this the shelter?" A timid voice spoke through the screened-in door.

"Hello, and yes," Charlotte replied, opening the door and standing aside so that the woman could walk in. She watched the taxi pull out of the driveway, knowing that the hospital had paid the fare.

The person at the door was petite, shorter than Charlotte, and carried a very small frame. She was still a teenager, her hair long and black and pulled tightly away from her face into a ponytail. There were bruises under both of her eyes, and she would not look directly at Charlotte. She walked in on crutches, with a plastic bag held under her right arm.

The absence of direct eye contact was familiar to Charlotte. She had grown accustomed to the shy ways that women greeted her when they came to the only place they had to stay. There was shame and embarrassment and sorrow and pain and lots of other things that Charlotte was never able to name. She just recognized it all when they all made those same first steps through the door and into their new lives.

"Welcome to St. Mary's," Charlotte said, smiling. She reached out to take the plastic bag from the woman.

"Rachel," the girl replied. "I'm Rachel." She handed over the bag immediately as if it had been required of her.

"I'm Charlotte," came the response. "Please come in and have a seat."

The young woman nodded and moved slowly into the living area and gingerly took a seat on the sofa. She sat toward the front of the cushions, appearing as if she was uncomfortable in a seated position. She held the crutches out beside her. Charlotte took them and placed them at her feet. Then she went over to a chair across from the sofa and sat down.

"Can I get you anything?" she asked.

Rachel shook her head.

"Have you had anything to eat today?"

She shook her head again. "I'm not so hungry."

Charlotte nodded. "Well, that's fine. But we do have some cake that someone made. I think it has fruit in it, creamy, very tasty. Maybe you'll like a piece later."

Rachel nodded in reply. She raised her eyes only enough to glance around the room.

"Is New Mexico your home, or did you move here from somewhere else?" Charlotte didn't want to ask too many questions to begin, but she thought some conversation might help ease the tension for the young woman.

"I'm from Texas." She hesitated. "I lived in Childress with my grandmother."

Charlotte nodded. She wasn't sure what to ask next. She thought about, *How did you get to Gallup and get tangled up in a violent relationship when you are so young?* or *How did you end up with bruises on your face and walking on crutches and moving to a women's shelter?* And yet she knew that wasn't really the best way to begin a relationship. She knew that Rachel's story would eventually come out. Charlotte was sure that once their newest client became comfortable in her surroundings, she would open up a little more.

"Well, why don't I round up some of the others

so that you can meet your housemates?" Charlotte asked, sounding as cheerful as she was able.

Rachel dropped her face again, and Charlotte got up and headed toward the back of the house. She found Maria, Loretta, and Loretta's youngest child in the rear bedroom. Sophia and Victoria were still working in the yard. She found Tempest on the phone in the kitchen. She gathered them all to tell them about Rachel and then asked them to join her in the introductions. She knew that Peggy, Lucille, and Anita were working and would meet their newest roommate at dinner.

The group of women walked into the living area and stood around Rachel. Each of them introduced themselves while Charlotte went into the bedroom that was being set up for Rachel. She saw the blowup mattress on the floor and knew it was a terrible way to offer hospitality to someone looking for shelter.

She walked back to the living room and motioned for Loretta. When she explained the situation, the mother of three was more than willing to help. Loretta would have one of her children sleep on the mattress and give the cot to the young woman.

Together the two women fixed the situation, and by the time Rachel was escorted to the room she would share with Sophia and Anita and Lucille, the middle bedroom, it looked as if they had been expecting her for weeks. The cot was situated in the corner with the other three single beds lined up beside it. It was tight conditions but it was certainly not unbearable.

After showing her around the house and the yard, the women left Rachel alone in the room to settle and to rest. Charlotte watched as they gathered in her office near the kitchen.

"How does somebody so young get beat up so bad?" Maria asked. She was in her sixties and had been volunteering at St. Mary's for almost three years. Her daughter had died from domestic violence, and she had vowed to work on her behalf, to help others who suffered the way her daughter and grandchildren had suffered.

"Don't she have family?" Loretta asked. "Is she even sixteen?" She was holding her baby in her arms.

"I think she's nineteen," Charlotte replied. "And no, I don't think there's any family. I'm sure she'll tell us about herself later."

"This a cruel world for a girl," Sophia noted, shaking her head. She had been in the shelter only a couple of weeks, but her injuries had not been quite as severe as Rachel's. She was one of the lucky ones.

There had been only one attack by her husband of five years. There had been several hard blows, directly across the face, but she had left him after that first time. Most women waited until there were three or four violent episodes. They didn't seek help until there were broken bones and medical interventions. Sophia was scared, just twenty-five, and didn't want to leave her husband. But she was smart and she had gotten out of the violent cycle early. She was at the shelter only until her sister could make room for her in California.

"We all attest to that fact," Victoria noted. She was the oldest of the residents, in her fifties, and she had been at St. Mary's the longest. She had run away from her husband in the middle of the night after a violent rape and beating. She had tried several times to leave him but always went back. She had all the scars to prove it. Finally, this last time she knew he would kill her, and she had decided that living without him was the only way she was going to live.

"You ain't never too young to be hit," Tempest responded. She was rubbing her neck, the scar from her boyfriend's knife still swollen and red on her narrow, brown neck.

Charlotte looked around at the women standing in her office and knew their stories. She knew their fear and their courage and their fierce loyalty to one another. She knew that she had not expected to find such a community for herself when she left North Carolina five years earlier.

She had only been a pastor in her professional career, and although she had loved being in that kind of community, it was nothing like the women's shelter. The closest she had come was the Hope Springs Cookbook Committee.

Beatrice, Margaret, Louise, and Jessie had been her teachers. They had taught her how to open her heart, how to share of herself, how to love deeply, how to be a friend. And that's how she thought of her work at the shelter, as being a friend. She glanced around at the women standing around her: Victoria, a sweet, unassuming housewife; Loretta, a loving mother; Sophia, a proud and strong young woman; and Tempest, the toughest of the group, the streetwise twenty-year-old, and Charlotte knew she was where she was meant to be.

"Well, let's go finish the yard work while it's still warm outside," Sophia said to Victoria.

"I can help," Tempest offered.

The older woman nodded and the three of them left. They all walked quietly by the room where Rachel was resting.

"I'm sorry we take up so much space and beds," Loretta said softly to Charlotte and Maria as she glanced down at the baby sleeping in her arms.

"Loretta, don't be crazy. This house would be so empty without Carmichael and Natasha and little Henry. We love that you are all here." Charlotte had sat down behind her desk.

Loretta glanced over to Maria. It appeared as if she needed more consolation.

"I'll get us another cot this evening. I know somebody who has one they don't use." Maria smiled and reached out and slid a finger across the baby's face. "I'm sorry if you heard me complaining. I have no right to say anything. I just . . ." She hesitated. "I just want everybody to have a good place to sleep and sometimes I just get overwhelmed here." She looked away. "*Señor, ten piedad*," she said in her native Spanish. "Father, have mercy."

Loretta nodded. "I know. I get overwhelmed too. And we really appreciate everything you do for us."

"I don't do anything," Maria confessed.

"Hey, you found the mattress, didn't you?" Charlotte said.

"And you brought us cake," Loretta added.

Maria smiled. "Has anybody even eaten any of it?" she asked.

Loretta glanced toward the kitchen. "I think I'll have a piece now." She nodded toward Charlotte. "Thanks for everything," she said.

Charlotte smiled as the woman and her baby left the office. She figured that Maria would join her but the other woman stood across from the desk.

"You okay?" Maria asked.

Charlotte didn't answer. She knew that Maria had a very sensitive side and was able to tell when someone was not feeling quite right.

"You had a phone call," Maria noted. "Is there something wrong at home?"

Charlotte blew out a breath. She knew that Maria

would pester her until she told her the truth. "It's one of my former parishioners. Margaret." She had mentioned the cookbook committee to Maria in previous conversations.

"The one who had breast cancer not too long ago?" Maria asked.

Maria had filled in for Charlotte during that hospitalization. Maria remembered how much the woman had meant to the executive director. She knew they were close.

Charlotte nodded.

"Is she okay?" Maria asked.

Charlotte waited and then shook her head. She glanced away, and Maria reached out and placed her hand on top of Charlotte's.

"Do you need to go back to North Carolina?" she asked, crossing herself. Maria was Catholic.

"No," Charlotte answered. "Not yet." She paused. "I mean, there's no real reason to at this point. She's going to start chemo next week. I'll go later."

Maria nodded. "We did fine without you last time," she noted, and winked when Charlotte looked up at her.

"I know. You are perfectly capable of running this place without me," Charlotte responded. "I just think I'll be needed more sometime later."

Maria pulled away her hand and cleared her throat. "Okay, but just let me know. I can rearrange some things at work and I can be here."

Charlotte studied her friend. Sometimes Maria would get carried away by details, like not having enough beds, but she really did make a difference with her work. Charlotte knew she wouldn't be able to do as much as she did without the help of Maria's volunteer work. It was a big job for just one person, and she was extremely grateful for what Maria gave to the shelter. She was like a mother to many of the residents at St. Mary's.

"Your offer means so much." Charlotte thought for a second. "And yes, if I change my mind, I will ask for your help."

Maria nodded. And the two women smiled.

"Now, what else can I do before I leave?"

Charlotte considered the question. "I think we've got today under control. I've got to fill out some forms for Rachel and try to finish that grant application, but everything seems to be fine for now."

"Did Tempest's boyfriend make bond?" Maria asked, knowing that Charlotte and Tempest had been worried that he would try to find her.

"No," Charlotte replied. "I called the DA and got it set pretty high. I don't think he'll be out for a while."

"Well, that's some good news, isn't it?"

"Yes," Charlotte responded. "There has been some of that today."

"Okay, I'll see you in the morning," Maria said. "I'll drop the cot off on my way to work. I won't be back to spend any time, though, until the weekend."

Charlotte nodded. She knew that Maria had lots of commitments at her work and her church and with her family. She was glad for the time she got from her volunteer and friend. "Thanks, Maria." She paused. "For everything."

"It's all good," Maria translated, and walked out of the office. "*Todo esta bien.*"

And Charlotte, knowing what she did about Margaret and now about a young woman with bruises and broken bones, wondered if such a thing could be true.

# Apple Dabble Cake

❄❄❄

3 eggs
2 cups sugar
1½ cups vegetable oil
3 cups flour
1 teaspoon baking soda
1 teaspoon salt
1 teaspoon cinnamon
3 cups chopped apples
1 cup chopped walnuts
1 teaspoon vanilla

Cream together eggs and sugar; add oil and mix well. Combine dry ingredients and add to oil mixture. Add chopped apples, nuts, and vanilla, mixing thoroughly. Spoon into a greased and floured tube pan and bake at 350 degrees for 80 minutes or until cake tests done.

[*continued*]

# SAUCE

½ stick margarine
1 cup brown sugar
¼ cup evaporated milk

Combine ingredients in saucepan over medium heat. Cook about 5 minutes. Pour over cooled cake.

# Chapter Seven

"Beatrice!" Louise was knocking on the bedroom window and shouting loudly. Her face was pressed squarely against the glass panes, her hands cupped around her eyes trying to see inside. She knocked again.

"Are you sure she's in there?" Jessie asked. She was glancing around the backyard, worried that a neighbor might think they were burglars. "Maybe we should just try calling again," she suggested.

"She won't answer the phone," Louise reminded her. "We tried that for an hour. I know she's in there."

"Beatrice, get out of bed. I can see you." She turned to Jessie, who was standing next to her. They had already tried calling on the cell phone, ringing the front doorbell, and knocking on the kitchen door. Beatrice had not answered.

"Besides, Dick said she wasn't going anywhere today, that she hadn't gone anywhere all week." Louise banged again on the window.

Jessie continued to look around nervously.

There was a small movement from the bedroom. Louise cupped her hands closer and squinted. She could see the bed and the sheets rumpled around what looked like a body underneath. She knew it was Beatrice and that she was trying to ignore them.

"She's moving," Louise noted to Jessie, who tried to see into the window at what Louise had noticed.

"Get up, Bea Witherspoon, or I'm going to call 911 and then you're going to have to face some ambulance driver in your nightgown."

The two women thought they heard something. Then Louise jumped when she saw a face right in front of hers. Bea was standing at the window and saying something but the words were muffled. Neither Jessie nor Louise could make it out, but they could both tell that she didn't appear very happy about the two women standing at her bedroom window.

"Go to the door!" Louise yelled. "Go open the back door!" She watched as Beatrice moved out of the bedroom.

She and Jessie hurried around the house to where she had directed Beatrice to meet them. All three of them arrived at exactly the same time. Louise and Jessie stood side by side on the landing.

"What do you want?" Beatrice asked, opening the door only a bit. She was still in her bed clothes. Her hair was a mess. She smoothed down the top of it with her hand.

"Good Lord, Bea," Louise addressed her friend as she pushed open the door and walked inside. "It is one o'clock in the afternoon. Have you not dressed yet?" she asked. She was staring at the woman before her as if she had never seen her looking as she did.

"I was taking a nap," Bea explained, moving away from the door and over to the sofa in the den. She sat down, yanking a blanket from the back of the sofa and pulling it around her.

"A nap?" Jessie asked, following Louise. She studied her friend. "Did you make any transition from waking up this morning to how you look now?"

Bea didn't answer. She glanced away at the two women as they sat down across from her in the overstuffed chairs she had bought to match the other new den furniture. Jessie and Louise didn't speak for a few minutes. Each was waiting for the other to begin.

They had decided a week ago that it was time for an intervention with Beatrice. She had missed the last two meetings of the cookbook committee and had not returned phone calls that both of them had made. She had gone with them to take Margaret for the outpatient surgery a few days earlier, but she had seemed sullen and withdrawn the entire time.

The two of them had spoken to Dick about her, and he confessed that he was at his wit's end with his wife. He had tried everything, he had told them, but Beatrice was not taking seriously what was happening and she was not getting any better. "If anything," he had said to Louise when they spoke earlier that morning, "she's getting worse." He was relieved to find out that Jessie and Louise were planning this visit. He had encouraged it.

Once the two of them were with their friend, however, neither one was sure of what exactly an intervention was. They had heard the term, thought they understood what it meant, but it felt different now that they were sitting across from the one whose life they were supposed to be intervening in.

Finally Jessie cleared her throat. "You want some coffee?" she asked as a way to begin.

Beatrice shook her head. Then she paused. "Do you?" she asked.

Jessie shook her head as well. They both glanced over to Louise, who seemed to be interested in the chair in which she was sitting. She was ignoring them.

Jessie began again. "Beatrice Newgarden Witherspoon, you have got to get yourself together." She delivered the opening proclamation. "There is something wrong with you and we are going to figure this thing out and get you fixed."

Beatrice seemed to expect what was being said.

"Do you know what is wrong?" Jessie asked. "Are you mad about something? Do you feel sad? Is it Dick or one of the children?" Clearly, no one understood what had happened to the perky and eternally optimistic Beatrice.

Bea smoothed down the sides of her hair again and pulled the blanket closer around her shoulders. She looked up at Jessie. She knew they were there for her benefit. She understood how much they cared for her, but she just didn't know what to say, how to respond.

"Just tell us when this started," Louise said as she sat back in the chair, waiting for some reply from Beatrice. She glanced around again at the chair and then slid her hands along the wide arms and appeared to be trying to get comfortable. "This is nice," she added, referring to the chair. "Is it new?"

"Louise, try to stay focused," Jessie said, and then turned back to Beatrice. "What happened to set you off like this?" she asked.

"I bought it in the summer at the outlet mall. I got it because it matched the sofa but it has some problems. Be careful. Dick and I don't sit in it that much. I think it's broken."

Louise nodded as she moved in the chair from side to side, leaning against the back, and sliding up and down in it.

"Beatrice, will you answer me?" Jessie asked, trying to keep the intervention in place.

Beatrice turned toward Jessie. She shrugged. "I don't know exactly."

"Is it something in your marriage?" Jessie asked.

Beatrice shook her head.

"Is it one of the girls?" she asked, referring to Beatrice's two daughters. "Teddy?"

Jessie hadn't heard that there was anything wrong with the two women, both of whom lived out of town or her son who was out of the country, but sometimes you didn't know everything about the children of friends unless you asked.

"No, they're all fine," Bea answered.

Jessie slumped in her chair. She was waiting for Louise to help in the conversation. She glanced over at her friend, and Louise was still moving around in the chair as if she was trying to get into a particular position.

"This is really a comfortable chair, Bea, is it a recliner?" Louise asked, paying no attention to what Jessie was doing. It was as if she had completely forgotten their purpose for this visit.

Jessie rolled her eyes. "Louise, could we stop talking about the chair?" she said with an agitated tone.

"Right, sorry," Louise apologized. She kept sliding her hands along the thick arms of the chair and then down along the sides. She was trying to see if there was a handle to change the chair's position.

"I don't think so," Bea responded. "But remember, be careful, it's broken."

"Right," Louise said, but she continued to move around in the chair.

"Louise," Jessie said sharply. She shot a hard look in the direction of Louise, who suddenly stopped what she was doing.

"Yeah, sorry," she said, moving her attention back to Beatrice.

"We know something is wrong, Bea," Jessie said, "and we're not leaving until we start to find some solution. You can't keep going like this. I mean, look at you."

Beatrice glanced down at herself. She pulled at the top of her nightgown. "I know," she said. "My mother would roll over in her grave if she saw me looking like this in the middle of the afternoon with guests in my house."

Louise shook her head. "We don't care about how you look, Bea," she said sympathetically. "We're just worried about you. You're just not yourself, and, well, we miss the old Bea."

Beatrice glanced over to her friend. She smiled. She was touched by her friend's concern. "Sometimes you used to get annoyed by the old Bea," she said.

"Most of the time, I got annoyed by the old Bea, it's true," Louise agreed. "But I still miss her."

"Is it Margaret?" Jessie finally asked the obvious. She knew all three of them were struggling with the same issues when it came to their friend.

"Maybe, a little," Beatrice replied. "But I don't know. I felt this way before we knew the cancer was back. But that did make it worse," she added.

Louise nodded. She had suffered too with the recent prognosis. She wasn't sleeping as well, and she noticed she had lost her appetite. Since she had taken over the cookbook project, she got nauseated every time she received a new recipe card from someone. She thought she was going to throw up when she got Emily Edwards's recipe for an apple dabble cake. She had not been able to add that one to the file on the computer yet. It had something to do with the sauce.

"What do you think about her?" Bea asked the two women.

Neither of them spoke at first. The truth was they hadn't really let themselves discuss it and they hadn't really thought that this conversation, this intervention, would go in this direction.

Jessie shook her head. "It doesn't look good," she replied. "Lana researched some stuff on the Internet about cancer spreading to the liver. There really isn't anything anybody can do about it. There's no surgery or anything. The chemo is the only treatment they've got. And I don't know if that really helps or not when the cancer has spread."

"She didn't do so well last time with the chemotherapy," Louise recalled.

The other women remembered Margaret's infection, her reaction to the harsh drugs, how sick she had been.

"Frankly, I was a little surprised that she agreed to take these treatments," Louise added.

Jessie nodded. "I'm not sure we gave her a chance to say no," she pointed out.

And all three women knew that was true. When the doctor had given the prognosis the three friends starting making the plans and appointments for the portacath surgery and the treatment dates while

Margaret got dressed. No one had even bothered to ask her if that was what she wanted.

"What will happen to her?" Louise asked. "What did Lana find out about what happens to somebody with liver cancer?"

Jessie looked down at her hands that she had folded and placed in her lap. "She didn't tell me much because I didn't really want to know. She just said a patient loses her appetite, stops eating, feels sick a lot."

The three women went silent. It was a while before anyone spoke again. Finally it was Beatrice who broke the tension. "I just feel like my whole life has been a joke," she confessed. "Like I've been the Hope Springs joke."

Louise and Jessie looked at each other. Both of them seemed surprised to hear what their friend was saying and startled to have the subject changed so quickly.

"I feel like I've been so stupid, trying to get people to do projects or join some group and that everybody goes home and laughs at me. 'Crazy ole Beatrice, always trying to fix something she broke.' " Beatrice dropped further down into the sofa.

"Fix something she broke?" Louise asked. "You didn't break anything," she added. "And what's wrong with caring enough about people that you try to offer them something to get better?"

There was no reply.

"I know I was the worst one about making fun of you and your projects, Bea." Louise leaned forward in Beatrice's direction. "But the truth is I was jealous that you had something to offer. I could never think of anything and you always had something. And maybe it was crazy or off the wall, but it was something and I was always envious of that."

"That's why this is so hard for us," Jessie continued. "We need you. We need your project and your ideas and your crazy expressions of faith. Especially now, especially with Margaret."

"Expressions of faith?" Beatrice asked. "You think they were expressions of faith?"

"Of course," Jessie replied. "Your cookbooks and your contests are a means to remind us to get up and do something, to see and act beyond ourselves and our own troubles. They bring us together and they are vehicles of grace. There is always more to them than what appears on the outside. It's like some offering that you make, and whenever you make an offering with a heart of love, it is always a gift that God can use to do what needs to be done."

"Wow," Beatrice exclaimed. "You really think that a cake cookbook is a vehicle of grace?"

"I don't think that," Louise noted with a smile. "I'm the one doing all of the work since you expressed your faith and then backed out, and I'm the one getting sick thinking about all these desserts. I don't feel any grace."

Jessie laughed. "Well, maybe I went over the top a little."

"I know what you're trying to do and I appreciate it, really I do." Beatrice smiled slightly. "But I just can't shake the feeling that I've never done anything great or meaningful. And now that Margaret is dying—" She stopped. The word surprised her, and she looked over at Jessie and Louise. They looked away.

"It's true, isn't it?" Beatrice asked. "That's really what's happening here, isn't it?"

No one answered.

"We don't know that," Louise finally replied.

"No, but it looks that way, doesn't it?" Jessie asked.

Beatrice and Louise didn't respond.

"In a sense, we're all dying," Beatrice remarked.

The two women glanced up at their friend. She was right and they knew it.

"Yeah," Jessie noted. "Margaret may just be going at it a little quicker than the rest of us."

"So, it's all that," Beatrice said. "It's Margaret dying and it's us getting old, and I look back on my life and feel like I've not done anything worthwhile, nothing important or meaningful. I feel like I've not made a difference in anybody's life."

Louise and Jessie were surprised to hear Beatrice's confession.

"Well, that's just stupid," Louise noted. The tone

of her voice was sharp, and it caused both women to turn quickly to her.

"I mean, really, Beatrice, you've not done anything meaningful?" She shook her head. "You really think that? That's what you really think?" She folded her arms across her chest. "Bea, you had three children!"

"So?" Beatrice asked.

"So?" Louise repeated. "You brought life into this world. There's no greater meaning than that."

Jessie looked over at Louise and, for the first time, wondered if her friend regretted not having children.

"Help me here, Jess," she said, not noticing the attention she was getting from her friend.

"She's right, Bea," Jessie said. "You have a husband who loves you. You've been a good friend to a lot of people."

Beatrice shrugged. "That doesn't feel very meaningful," she said.

"Well, I don't know of any more meaningful act in a person's life than to be a friend," Louise responded. "You share of your heart. You love. That's the only meaning that matters."

Jessie nodded. "She's right, Bea. Everything else, all the things people call great, none of those are anywhere near as meaningful as having love."

"Maybe," Beatrice said.

"Maybe nothing," Louise shot back.

"So, that's what all this depression and staying in bed and acting all withdrawn is about?" Jessie asked. "You think you've never done anything meaningful?"

Beatrice nodded. "That and I quit taking the hormones the doctor prescribed."

Jessie and Louise looked at each other.

"Why did you do that?" It was Jessie who asked the question.

"I just thought I didn't need them anymore," Bea replied.

"Well, clearly that's a mistake," Louise said.

"Okay, so, we get you some more estrogen and we find you a purpose, then you'll be better?" Jessie asked.

Beatrice nodded with a smile. "That should do it," she said, trying to make herself believe that was enough to fix everything.

"That's great," Louise said, and pushed hard against the back of the chair.

Beatrice and Jessie turned just as she fell back and flipped over.

# Granny Causey's Light Fruitcake

❄❄❄

1 pound butter
2 cups sugar
12 eggs
4 cups flour
1 teaspoon baking powder
2 pounds diced cherries
2 pounds diced pineapple
1 pound mixed fruit
8 ounces figs
8 ounces dates
2 cups nuts

Cream butter and sugar. Add eggs one at a time, beating well after each addition. Combine flour and baking powder and add to creamed mixture (reserving small amount for dredging fruit). Combine fruits and nuts, then dredge with flour. Carefully fold fruits into creamed mixture. Grease and line 2 tube pans with wax paper. Spoon mixture evenly into pans. Bake at 250 degrees for 3 to 5 hours.

# Chapter Eight

Jessie and Beatrice helped Louise up from the floor and placed the chair back in its proper position.

"Still comfortable?" Jessie asked, laughing.

"Very funny," Louise said as she pulled herself up to the sofa.

"I told you, Lou, the thing is broken," Beatrice noted again. She had dropped the blanket from around her and was standing in her nightgown.

"Yes, you did tell me that. But what I don't understand is why would a person buy a broken chair?" Louise asked, dusting herself off.

"It matches," Jessie said, recalling what Bea had told them earlier in the conversation. It seemed to make perfect sense to her as well.

"Let me go put my clothes on," Beatrice said.

She walked around Jessie and into her bedroom. She yelled from where she was, "Fix yourselves something to drink if you like."

Jessie and Louise headed into the kitchen and opened the refrigerator. Jessie took out a pitcher of tea while Louise found three glasses, found ice in the freezer, and filled all three to the top.

"You think this helped?" Jessie asked Louise.

"She's out of bed, isn't she?" Louise responded.

Jessie raised her eyebrows and nodded.

"That has to count for something," Louise added. She took a sip from her tea. She shook her head. "Imagine Beatrice worried about having a life with no meaning."

Jessie sat down on one of the kitchen barstools. "I know, it surprised me too."

"Where does she come up with these crazy notions?" Louise asked.

"Well, I don't think it's a crazy notion," Jessie replied. "It's a fair question to ask about one's life. I've asked it, haven't you?" She looked over to her friend, who was standing at the sink.

Louise turned to Jessie. "I don't know. I guess I don't think those kind of deep thoughts. I get up in the morning. I do what has to be done. I eat. I sleep. I get up and do it again."

"Do you wish you had had children?" Jessie asked, remembering what Louise had said to Bea.

Louise leaned against the sink. She placed her glass of tea beside her. "I don't think so," she replied. "It just never seemed like it was in the cards for me, you know. Like love too, I guess."

Jessie didn't respond. She thought of Roxie, the woman who lived with Louise in the final months of her life. She had been the love of Louise's life and everyone knew it. Only Roxie had married and had children. It was an unrequited love.

"Oh, you've had love," Jessie said. "Your friendship is fierce, Louise Fisher. I daresay your love is the strongest of us all."

Louise smiled. She tilted her head and winked at Jessie. "I do love my friends," she noted. "But I wouldn't say that my love was any stronger than yours or Margaret's or Bea's. We're pretty lucky to have each other."

Jessie nodded.

Immediately they both thought about Margaret, about the conversation they had just shared, the things that had finally surfaced.

"She's not really dying, is she?" Louise asked.

Jessie sighed. "We don't know," she said. "Not yet, not now."

"But I think if we're really her friends, then we ought to think about that, figure that out."

"What's there to figure out?" Bea asked. She had put on a running suit. Her hair had been combed and she looked almost like her old self.

"Well, look at that. I think I'm going to advertise my services as an intervention specialist. We turned a bed-bound, depressed, sad-looking human being into a super jock." Louise applauded.

"I'm wearing comfortable pants that happen to have a matching jacket. I seriously doubt you can call me a super jock," Bea responded.

"Well, whatever you call yourself, you look a lot better," Jessie said.

"That image of you in that sorry old nightgown standing over me is one I hope I can shake," Louise said as she handed Beatrice a glass of tea.

"That's a fairly new nightgown," she replied. "It's from Macy's."

Louise gave a look of surprise. "I'm just saying that image is not your finest moment."

Beatrice took a drink and sat down next to Jessie. "Whatever . . ." she said. "Now what are you trying to figure out?" Bea asked.

"Margaret," Jessie answered.

"What's there to figure out?" Bea asked innocently. "Margaret never seems upset about anything. She looks like she's handling this better than the rest of us."

"That's the thing about Margaret," Jessie noted. "She always seems like she's handling everything; but this time she may need some help."

"You think she knows?" Louise asked.

"Margaret?" Jessie asked. "Margaret knows better than anyone."

The women thought about their friend. Louise and Beatrice agreed with Jessie. They all three assumed that Margaret understood what was happening in her body.

"Well, I'm going to get back on my estrogen and I'm going to do better with Margaret and with you two," Beatrice promised.

"You gonna take over the cookbook?" Louise asked.

"Are you having some particular difficulty in collecting the recipes?" Beatrice asked with a smile. Even in her depression, she had found some enjoyment in considering that Louise was running that project.

"Did you get Jan Causey's grandmother's recipe?" Jessie asked. She suddenly remembered the message she had gotten on her phone at home. She had returned the call and given the caller Louise's number.

"Granny Causey's fruitcake?" Louise asked. She nodded, taking a big swig of her tea. "Got it."

"What kind of fruit does she use?" Beatrice asked. She squinted her eyes at Louise.

"I don't know what kind of fruit she uses," Louise replied. "I just got it in the mail and typed it with the others."

"You type the recipes on your computer and you don't read over the ingredients?" Beatrice asked, sounding surprised. "How do you know if they're right?"

"I don't care if they're right or not," Louise replied. "I just stick them in there the way they come."

Beatrice blew out a breath, making a kind of whishing noise. "I can't believe that I turned this project over to you and that you aren't checking out these recipes. Suppose something is wrong in one of them?" she asked. The look of exasperation was undeniable. "Help me out here, Jessie."

Jessie shrugged. "What?" she asked.

"You don't think you should bake the cakes following the directions of the recipes before we publish them in a book with the name of our church on it?"

Louise looked over at Jessie. Clearly, neither of them had thought about this. Louise folded her arms across her chest. "You tried out all of those recipes in the first cookbook before you sent them to the printer?"

"Of course!" Beatrice replied. "How else do you know if they work?"

"I don't care if they work," Louise responded. "I didn't agree to bake fifty cakes when I said I would help you out on this."

"Well, if I had known how frivolously you were going to carry out this project, I would certainly never have allowed myself to drop down into the well of sorrow. I thought that at the very least, I could count on you to do a professional job!" Beatrice sounded hurt.

"You made all those recipes from that first book?" Jessie asked, sounding just as surprised as Louise. "Lord, Bea, I'd be depressed too if I thought I was going to have to bake all those cakes."

"That's not depressing," Bea said, turning to face Jessie. "That's just part of the job."

"Well, maybe it's part of the way you do the job, but not me." Louise shook her head. "Besides, have you managed to take care of your assignment in this project?"

Beatrice's face turned a bright shade of red.

"You haven't, have you?" Louise asked in astonishment.

"What was she supposed to do?" Jessie asked.

"Beatrice, we've got to have a prize in the next couple of weeks. I've promised all these women that you're working on something wonderful. They all think they're going to be featured in some restaurant at Christmas. You haven't gotten anybody to agree to sponsor this thing?"

"I've got something," Beatrice said innocently.

"What?" Louise asked.

"You could try Lester's Barbecue Shack. They could use a new dessert. The last time James and I ate there, they had some awful store-bought banana pudding." Jessie was trying to be helpful.

"I tried Lester," Beatrice responded. She just shook her head and made a kind of face.

"What have you got?" Louise asked again.

"It's something real special," Beatrice replied with a noticeable bit of hesitation. "I just got a few more phone calls to make and it will be official."

"Beatrice, you are a terrible liar," Louise said.

"I am offended by that, Louise Fisher," Beatrice said. "You take over this cookbook and suddenly you're acting like a little Hitler."

"Bea, don't try to sweet-talk your way out of this. What's your real special prize for the winning recipe?"

Beatrice raised her chin and turned away from

Louise. "I'm getting the winner a chance to be on television."

"Oh, you are not," Louise snapped. She turned to Jessie, shaking her head in disbelief. "Jessie, do you think Lester would provide a prize or support us somehow?"

"I don't see why not. He needs more business and I don't see how it could hurt anything for him to advertise that he was serving the winning cake. What would he have to do?"

"Let's see. We could make him the official judge and then he could just add an insert in his menu announcing the cake." Louise was trying to think of everything that would have to be done.

"He'd have to bake a few of the cakes, though, wouldn't he?" Jessie was considering the dilemma as well.

Beatrice cleared her throat, trying to enter the conversation. She was shocked to hear the two women completely ignoring her work in arranging the contest prize.

"Maybe we could offer to bake the cakes for him?" Jessie asked Louise.

"We could get some of the churchwomen to bake them."

"I said that I have arranged a prize!" Beatrice interrupted the conversation.

Both of the women looked over to Beatrice. Clearly they didn't believe her.

"You've found some cooking show host to agree

to have a person from Hope Springs Community in North Carolina appear on their show to demonstrate how to bake a Christmas cake?" Louise went straight to the heart of the matter.

"Well, I didn't say it was a cooking show," Beatrice said softly.

"A local morning news program then?" Louise offered.

"Channel Eight?" Jessie asked. "That would be nice. They have a cooking segment at about five-thirty A.M., I think. That's lovely, Beatrice."

"You called FOX News?" Louise asked. "In Greensboro?" She sounded as if she didn't believe what she was hearing.

"Well, no, not exactly," Beatrice replied.

The two women waited for Beatrice to explain. She was silent.

"What then?" Louise asked.

"It's that cable channel, isn't it?" Jessie asked. "That community access channel way up there in the sixties. That's still nice," she added. "It will be very special to the winner."

"Is that it?" Louise asked.

Beatrice shook her head.

"Channel Two?" Jessie asked.

Another negative gesture from Beatrice.

"Forty-five over in Winston?" Jessie asked. "But they don't even do local broadcasting anymore, do they?"

"No," Louise replied.

"It's Twelve, isn't it?" Jessie asked. She was hoping that Beatrice would jump in at some point and explain her plan. "The NBC affiliate, that's perfect, Bea!"

"Is it Twelve?" Louise asked.

"No."

"Are you going to tell us?" Louise asked.

"I wrote that young woman who has her own baking show. It comes on in the afternoon, after Oprah."

Jessie and Louise tried to figure out the show to which Beatrice was referring.

"I thought Dr. Phil came on after Oprah," Louise noted.

"No, not anymore. It's the news that comes on after her. She's on at four P.M. and then there's the five o'clock news," Jessie said.

"Not on the same channel," Beatrice explained. "On that food channel."

Louise shrugged. It was obvious that she didn't know about the food channel or any of its shows.

"You got the Cake Lady?" Jessie asked, sounding very surprised.

Beatrice made a sort of coughing noise. She clearly didn't want to answer.

"Beatrice, that's incredible. The Cake Lady is going to host the winner of our little contest?"

"Who's the Cake Lady?" Louise wanted to know.

"Who's the Cake Lady?" Jessie repeated the question. "She's the baker to the stars. She's famous! Everybody's heard of the Cake Lady!"

"Well, maybe everybody but me," Louise announced. "Why is she so famous?"

"She does birthday cakes that have all these elaborate scenes painted in the icing. She makes some that look like animals and dolls. She does all the celebrity wedding cakes. She does one that looks like a castle that has a waterfall in it. She's amazing. How on earth did you get her to agree to judge our little contest, Bea?" Jessie wanted to know. "That's just fantastic," she added before Beatrice could answer. "I may just have to find a recipe myself. I would love to meet her!"

Beatrice made that coughing noise again.

"Will she come here or will the winner go to her studio?" Jessie asked.

"I just asked her to judge." Beatrice finally spoke.

"Yeah, that's right. How silly to think she would show the winner on her television program. But still, this is just unbelievable," Jessie said. She shook her head and finished drinking her tea. "Think about how proud one of our women would be to know her cake was judged by the Cake Lady?"

Beatrice smiled nervously. She could feel Louise's eyes on her. She fidgeted with the collar of her jacket.

"You wrote the Cake Lady?" Louise asked Beatrice.

"Yep," she replied.

"And you asked her to judge our little cake recipe contest?"

"I did."
"And the Cake Lady agreed?" Louise was getting to the bottom of this, and fast.
"Unbelievable," Jessie said again. "The women are going to be thrilled."
"And the Cake Lady agreed?" Louise asked again.
"That is beautiful, Beatrice, just beautiful."
"Well, she didn't exactly agree," Beatrice confessed.
Louise nodded. She leaned back against the sink.
"Would you two like some pie?" Beatrice jumped up from her seat and walked over to the refrigerator. "I think we have some chocolate left over from Dick's family reunion."
"We're talking about cakes, Bea." Louise sounded impatient.
"I don't have any cake," Beatrice responded politely. "But Dick says this pie is really good. I didn't have any, on account of being depressed and all."
"Beatrice, did the famous cake woman agree to judge our contest?"
"Well, not exactly," Beatrice answered. "But she did agree to read my letter," she added as if this was something important.
"Ah, Bea," Jessie said, sounding disappointed.
"I called her studio and her assistant, well, actually I think it was the assistant to the assistant, but he promised me that he would make sure that she got the letter. He was in charge of her mail."

Louise rolled her eyes. "Why do you think a famous baker would care about our little contest?" she asked.

"Because she bakes cakes and our contest is for a cake recipe, a Christmas cake recipe. It's right up her alley!" Beatrice exclaimed.

Louise sighed. "Jessie, can you call Lester and ask him if he would be the judge and feature the cake for one night at his restaurant?"

Jessie nodded. She was disappointed.

"I will not have the winner of this contest having their cake eaten in a barbecue shack!" Beatrice slammed the pie plate on the counter. "I said that I would handle the prize and I am going to do it! The Cake Lady is going to judge the contest!"

"Bea, it's almost Thanksgiving. That means Christmas is just a month away. If this woman hasn't agreed to judge this contest by now, she isn't going to do it. It's the holidays. She isn't going to want to mess with this during the holidays."

"I said that I would handle it!"

"Bea, Louise is right. It's too late now. Just let us handle this. You call your doctor and get you some estrogen. It's fine. Nobody knows the prize anyway." Jessie was trying to smooth things between her two friends.

"Well, actually they do now," Beatrice said timidly.

"What?" Louise asked.

"I happened to mention this to Betty Mills over at the funeral home."

"Flapping Tongue Betty?" Louise sounded outraged. "There's probably an ad in the paper by now!"

"She was giving me another hard time about our contest and our little church and how we couldn't afford a good prize like the Episcopalians and I just got tired of it."

"So you told her the Cake Lady is going to judge our contest?" Louise dropped her head in her hands. "Beatrice, really, what is wrong with you?"

"Well, how do I know? You should be the one who can answer that. You're the ones who were supposed to be bringing me an invention!"

"It's intervention. And I'm not sure it can help. Now, could I please have a piece of pie?" Louise glanced over to Jessie, and the two women simply shook their heads.

# Peaches and Cream Cake

❄❄❄

1 18½ ounce butter-flavor cake mix
1½ cups sugar
4 tablespoons cornstarch
4 cups chopped fresh peaches
½ cup water
2 cups whipping cream
2 to 3 tablespoons powdered sugar
1 cup sour cream
fresh sliced peaches

Prepare cake according to directions, using 2 8-inch cake pans. Cool and split each layer. Combine sugar and cornstarch in saucepan and add peaches and water. Cook over medium heat, stirring constantly until smooth and thick. Cool completely. Combine whipping cream and powdered sugar. Beat until stiff peaks form. Spoon one third peach filling over split layers. Spread one third sour cream over filling. Repeat procedures on layers. Frost with sweetened whipped cream and garnish with fresh sliced peaches.

# Chapter Nine

"Peaches and cream cake?" Margaret had taken her seat in a large recliner in the treatment area of the cancer center at the hospital. She was there for her second chemotherapy treatment. She was waiting for the nurse. Louise had tossed a blanket across her legs. She was facing out the window. "That doesn't sound very much like Christmas."

"I know it but that's the recipe that Dorothy wanted to enter." Louise was standing next to Margaret. She was holding a red stocking that one of the volunteers had given them when they came in.

"There's a candy cane in here, you want it?" She pulled it out and showed Margaret.

Margaret shook her head. "No, you eat it."

Louise shrugged and stuck it back in the stocking. She could see that there were other pieces of candy inside and what looked to be a card bearing a message of goodwill. Apparently some church had made the gifts for all the cancer patients.

"You figure out a prize yet?" Margaret asked. She slid over in her chair a bit.

Louise could see that she was anxious. She wondered if her friend was in some kind of pain or if she was just nervous about the treatment.

“Beatrice told me that she was handling it so I’m staying out of that part.” She paused, concerned about how Margaret was acting. “I’m just collecting the recipes and typing them up. She said that she was arranging for the prize so I am staying out of her way. Besides, she is grouchy since they haven’t been able to get her hormones adjusted.” She hesitated again. “You okay?” she asked.

Margaret nodded, although it wasn’t very convincing.

“Mrs. Peele, how are you today?” A nurse had walked up and was getting the medicine bags ready. She was pulling an IV pole with her. She was young, looked like a teenager, and was wearing a lab coat with reindeer and snowmen stenciled on it.

“Ready to get this behind me,” Margaret replied.

“I understand,” the nurse responded. “These are not much fun, I know,” she added.

Louise smiled. “Nice coat,” she said, and then moved out of the way as the nurse put on her gloves and prepared to start the treatment.

“ ’Tis the season, right?” the young nurse asked as she swabbed the area above Margaret’s chest and inserted the needle into the portacath under Margaret’s skin.

Louise noted how Margaret flinched when the needle went in. She reached out and placed her hand on top of Margaret’s as the nurse finished. “You okay?” she asked.

Margaret nodded, but she kept her eyes closed. Louise had sensed all morning that Margaret wasn't acting herself. Something seemed different about her, but Louise hadn't asked. She was afraid to ask.

"All right," the nurse said as she punched in buttons on the machine. "I'll check in just a few minutes to make sure everything is okay." Then she patted Margaret on the shoulder. "Does it feel like it's supposed to?" she asked, and then smiled as Margaret nodded.

"Okay, push the red button if you need me," she instructed the patient, referring to the nurse's call button on the large remote that hung next to the chair.

Louise pulled a chair next to Margaret and they both looked out the window. There was a large garden area behind the cancer center. Volunteers had planted small fruit trees and different kinds of flowers. There were several stone sculptures, mostly angels, a few squirrels and rabbits. There were four bird feeders close by, and all of them were full of seed.

The garden was strategically located for cancer patients to observe as they sat and received treatment. Margaret had said before that she thought it was a nice idea but that it still didn't do much to ease the sting of needles, cover up the smell of the hospital, or distract anyone from the idea that they were fighting their hardest battle.

"Still," she had noted once to Louise, "it's better than some television show blaring at them."

"You want something to drink?" Louise asked.

Margaret shook her head.

"You want headsets to listen to music?" she asked, reaching into her bag to pull out the CD player she always brought with them.

Again, Margaret shook her head.

"You want to talk?" Louise asked, even though she hoped Margaret didn't.

Jessie had told Louise that they all needed to spend some time with Margaret letting her talk about things, about how she felt and about what she wanted, but Louise had not been able to start or even allow for such a conversation. She wasn't ready and she knew it.

Margaret waited and then shook her head again. She reached out and took Louise by the hand. "I don't feel much like talking today."

Louise nodded, relieved.

The two women sat in silence for a few minutes, and then Louise noticed that Margaret began to fidget in her chair. "You okay?" she asked.

Margaret didn't answer. She struggled as she tried to change her sitting position and then flinched when it appeared as if the IV line got caught.

"Is something wrong with the needle?" Louise asked. "Do you want me to get the nurse?" She stood up beside Margaret.

Margaret shook her head.

This was her second treatment since the new prognosis, and she was having some difficulty in receiving the medication. One slight infection had already occurred at the IV site after the first treatment, and she had been sick for a couple of days.

The doctor had suggested that they might have to replace the portacath. Margaret hated the thought of another surgery, so she had not complained about the infection and was hopeful that this treatment would go more smoothly. They had already postponed it an extra week, and she just wanted to get through with them. She was scheduled for six and was supposed to be finished just after New Year's Day.

"No, it just feels a little different. I'm sure it's okay." She closed her eyes and thought a distraction might help. "Okay, let's talk. So, what about Beatrice?" she asked.

"It's nothing," Louise replied, recognizing that the treatment was difficult for her friend. "Just rest."

Margaret didn't argue. She was trying to make things better for herself; but she was tired and uncomfortable and she had been right the first time, she didn't really feel like talking. She knew that Louise didn't expect to be entertained so she tried to do what her friend had suggested and rest. After a few minutes more, however, she couldn't stand the discomfort any longer.

"I think you're going to have to get the nurse. Something just doesn't feel right."

Louise pulled Margaret's blouse away from the site to see for herself. The site just below her collarbone was red and swollen. When the hospital had scheduled the appointment, Louise had thought it was too soon for another treatment; but she had not said anything because she wanted Margaret to get through with them too. Now she was angry at herself for letting Margaret go through this ordeal. She placed the blouse back and walked over to the nurses' station. The doctor was called, and it wasn't long before the IV was pulled.

By five o'clock that afternoon, Margaret was in a room on the oncology unit of the hospital. The portacath had been surgically removed and she was being given high doses of antibiotics. Jessie and Beatrice had met Louise at the hospital, and all three of the friends went into the waiting room just around the corner from where Margaret was sleeping.

"What exactly did the doctor say?" Jessie asked Louise as they pulled chairs out and sat together around the table.

"He said that he didn't think that they could put the contraption back in again." Louise rubbed her hand across the side of her face. She was tired from the long day of waiting and she hadn't eaten since breakfast.

As if she had been asked by Louise to get her something to eat, Beatrice walked over to the vending machine behind where they sat. She dropped in four quarters and selected some juice for her friend. Then she reached into her purse and pulled out a pack of crackers and an apple. She set them on the table in front of Louise.

"Eat something," she said.

"Yes ma'am," Louise responded. She opened the crackers and took one. She offered them to Jessie and then to Beatrice. Both women shook their heads. They had both eaten already and were not hungry.

Louise glanced up and noticed how much better Beatrice appeared. "You see your doctor?" she asked her friend. "You get your woman juices straightened out?"

Beatrice stood up, turned around, and pulled at the waistband of her pants. She turned her head around, making sure that Jessie and Louise had seen what she was showing them, a small patch stuck just above her right hip, and then pulled her pants back up and sat down. "I am clearheaded and no longer hysterical or overwrought," she announced.

"Estrogen patch, that's nice, Beatrice," Louise noted. "And I think the old man across the hall really liked the show."

Beatrice glanced out the door and then realized that Louise was only teasing her.

"See how much better you are?"

"Dr. Linden said I could probably use a little testosterone too. It seems that the older we get the less we have of that hormone too. But I said I didn't want to take that because I already had a little mustache."

Jessie and Louise looked confused.

"Testosterone?" Bea asked. "That's the manly hormone," she said. "You probably won't ever need any of that one," she noted to Louise with a slight smile.

"What else did the doctor say?" Jessie had turned back to Louise. Neither of the two women wanted to have any more conversation with Beatrice about her hormones.

"He said that she wouldn't be able to have the portacath back in that same spot but that they would probably be able to put one in her arm." Louise munched on a cracker.

"I don't have a mustache," she said to Beatrice, suddenly considering what Bea had implied.

"I didn't say you did," Beatrice responded.

"You said that I probably wouldn't have to take testosterone," she added.

"Forget what Bea said," Jessie instructed. "When did this happen?" she asked. "Was she already taking the treatment?"

Louise nodded. "She didn't seem to act right when the nurse started it. I don't think the needle ever went in correctly. I think she still had some infection."

Jessie shook her head. She knew how much pain her friend had been in. She had tried to get her to put off the appointment for another week, but Margaret had seemed determined to go through with it.

"When can she go home?" Beatrice asked.

"In the morning if she feels like it," Louise replied. She took a sip from her juice. "But the doctor thought she should stay," she noted. "I think he wants her to finish the treatment. They had to stop it before she got the full dosage."

"She's got an infection," Jessie said. "She doesn't need any more of that mess in her system right now."

"I know, but he thinks she needs to stay on schedule as much as she can. He also wanted to know if she might take a bone marrow transplant."

"He just can't accept that she's this sick," Jessie responded. "He wants to think he can cure her."

Louise shook her head and ate another cracker.

"Did she say anything before they had to take it out?" Beatrice asked.

"Just that she was tired and didn't think she could do this anymore," Louise replied.

"She's already been through so much," Jessie added. "I just don't think she wants any more of this."

"If she quits taking the treatments, then she's giving up," Beatrice said.

"So, what's wrong with that?" Jessie asked.

"Besides, who says these treatments are doing anything for her anyway?"

Louise and Beatrice didn't answer.

"Did she say anything about quitting?" Bea asked.

Louise shook her head. "But I don't think she wants this," she added. "I mean, at first, I think she was okay about it, but now, after the infection, I don't think this is what she wants."

"Then why is she doing it?" Beatrice wanted to know.

"For us," Jessie replied. "It's like we said a couple of weeks ago. When the doctor told her that the cancer was back, we didn't give her a chance to make her mind up. We arranged these treatments for her. We made her schedule these appointments. No one ever asked her what she wanted. She's doing this for us."

"Then maybe we need to let her stop," Beatrice said. "Maybe somebody needs to tell her she doesn't have to do this anymore."

"I'm not telling her that," Louise said. Her voice was stretched and thin. "She can't stop. Jessie, you know what it means if she stops."

Jessie reached out and took Louise by the hand.

"She can get over this infection and we can try again in January," Louise said as she pushed the crackers and juice away from her.

Jessie glanced over at Beatrice, and both of the women looked at their friend.

"Lou, it's in her liver," Beatrice said softly.

"So?" Louise asked, pulling her hand away from Jessie. "She can get a liver transplant. If they give them to drunks, they can give one to her."

Jessie sat back against her chair. Louise had been acting like she was fine with everything that was going on with Margaret, but Jessie knew it was just that, acting.

"I just think it's time to let Margaret talk, to let her make up her own mind about what she wants," Jessie said. She leaned in again to Louise. "You don't want her sick like this, do you?" she asked. "You didn't want that for Roxie?" she added. "Did you?"

"That was different," Louise shot back. "Roxie didn't have her mind. She wasn't herself. Margaret is . . ." She paused. "Margaret is . . ."

"Margaret can make up her mind and she needs us to let her do that. She deserves to have her friends let her do that." Jessie had taken a very serious tone.

Louise shook her head. "She can just go home and we'll take care of her, get her body strong and give her time to get better; and then they can put the portacath somewhere else and she can take the treatments through January and be better by spring."

Beatrice slid her chair closer to Louise. She reached out and took both of her friend's hands in hers. She looked her squarely in the eyes. "She is not going to be better by spring, Louise. The cancer has spread in her liver and is probably in other places as well."

Jessie sat up and joined Beatrice. "Margaret needs us now more than ever," she said. "But she doesn't need us in that way of denial and avoidance. She needs us to be okay and to let her know that we will support her and care for her no matter what she chooses to do. She needs to know that she can make a decision about what she wants to do with the rest of her life without worrying about us."

"I'm not okay," Louise said, the tears welling in her eyes. "Do you know that?" she asked. "I'm not okay."

Jessie nodded. "I know," she responded. "I'm not okay yet either." She reached down in her purse and brought out tissues for all three of them. "But I'm working on it," she added. "I'm working on it because I know that's what Margaret needs the most."

Louise nodded, knowing that what her friend was saying was true. She had known it for some time. "Okay, I'll try, but I can't promise you anything."

Beatrice leaned across the table and patted Louise on the hand. "I thought the same thing when you came over and brought the invention to me. But now look how much better I am."

"Bea," Louise said as she took a tissue from

Jessie and wiped her eyes. “It’s intervention, not invention. And I’m glad your hormones are making you feel better but I’m afraid it’s going to take more than just a patch on my butt to help me with this.”

“Maybe not a patch,” Beatrice answered. “Maybe more like a kick.” And she reached over with a wink and took the last cracker from Louise.

# Fran's Fresh Coconut Cake

❄❄❄

½ cup butter
½ cup shortening
1 teaspoon vanilla
1 teaspoon lemon extract
2⅔ cups sugar
3½ cups flour
1½ teaspoons baking powder
¼ teaspoon salt
1 cup milk
5 eggs

In a large mixing bowl, cream butter, shortening, vanilla, and lemon extract. Sift together dry ingredients. Combine flour mixture, milk, and eggs with shortening, about one third at a time, saving 2 eggs until last to add to batter. Bake in 3 greased and floured 9-inch pans at 325 degrees for 30 minutes or until done.

[*continued*]

## ICING

2 cups sugar
½ cup boiling water
1 cup quartered marshmallows
2 egg whites
⅛ teaspoon baking powder
pinch salt
1 teaspoon vanilla
1 fresh coconut, grated

Cook sugar and water until it reaches a temperature of 245 degrees. Add marshmallows and stir until they are melted. Remove from heat. Beat egg whites until stiff; then pour sugar mixture into whites, beating as you pour. Continue beating, adding baking powder, salt, and vanilla until stiff enough to spread on cake. Spread icing on layers, then add grated coconut between each layer. Repeat for top and sides.

# Chapter Ten

"Thank you, Frances, this is a lovely surprise and it's my favorite." Margaret took the cake from her neighbor.

She could see that it was coconut, and she knew how good Frances Martin's coconut cakes were. In fact, she had told Louise to ask Frances for the recipe to put into the cookbook. She thought coconut cake was a perfect Christmas cake, much better than some of the entries that had been submitted. "Please, come in, it's so cold out there." She held open the door.

"I know a whole cake is a lot for just one person." Frances walked in. "But you can freeze it for later." The woman paused, thinking about how to rephrase what she was suggesting. "Or, um, you can just share it with the people who have been staying with you."

She stood just inside the door, her back up against the wall. She knew that hospice was now in charge of Margaret's care. She had seen the nurses and other staff members coming and going from her neighbor's house.

The woman appeared awkward and uncomfortable. She and Margaret had been neighbors for more than twenty years, going in and out of each other's houses a million times; but now the neighbor appeared as if she didn't know how even to talk to her old friend.

She had heard the gossip about Margaret's condition and she had kept putting off a visit since Margaret had come home from the hospital. Finally, having stayed away for more than a couple of weeks and knowing that she was leaving that afternoon for the entire month of December to be with her family in Florida, and after getting the call from Louise about the recipe, Frances had baked a coconut cake and gone to see her neighbor.

Once she was there, she felt very much out of place. Secretly, she had hoped that someone else would answer the door and that she wouldn't have to see Margaret. But once her neighbor answered the door, she realized that she was going to have to stay a few minutes and act sociable.

"Let me take your coat, Frances." Margaret placed the cake on the table by the door and reached for the woman's coat.

"Oh, okay, thank you," and she slipped out of her thick jacket, still standing close to the door. She watched Margaret as she hung the coat in the closet. She could tell that her neighbor had lost more weight in the last few weeks. She looked frail and her skin had a yellow cast to it. That would be because of the liver involvement, Frances thought.

"I guess they're calling for some bad weather this evening," she said as a means to conversation.

"That's what they just said on the morning

report," Margaret responded. She was moving very slowly and was demonstrating some difficulty in hanging the coat. Frances wasn't sure how to offer assistance.

"Would you like some coffee?" Margaret asked. She was able to get the coat hung, and she closed the closet door and picked up the cake to take into the kitchen.

"Yes, that would be nice. Here." Frances reached out. "Let me take that in there for you."

Margaret nodded and the two women headed out of the front room. Margaret walked slowly and tentatively as her neighbor followed behind.

"I've missed seeing you," Margaret noted as she gestured toward the counter for a place for Frances to set the cake and then pulled out two mugs from the dish drain and started fixing their drinks. "I thought you might have already gone on your trip."

"No, I'm, uh . . . I've been busy with my volunteering and I, um, just haven't gotten around to visit like I used to. I leave this afternoon. Do you want me to help you with that?" She was standing behind her neighbor and she could see that Margaret was weak. Frances fidgeted with the sleeves on her blouse.

Margaret knew that her neighbor was uncomfortable. She had seen this reaction quite often since she had come home from the hospital. Many of her church friends and neighbors had stayed away at first, and then once they started visiting, they seemed more like strangers than friends.

She wasn't sure what news was being shared about her but she was certainly aware that everyone was acting differently around her. She guessed that they all thought she was dying in a couple of days; and maybe she was, she didn't know. All she knew since coming home from the hospital and discontinuing the treatments was that she didn't feel that great but she certainly didn't feel like she was dying.

It didn't concern her that much, however. She understood that hearing that a friend or acquaintance was terminal made everyone uncomfortable. In the past, she had acted the same way around her friends who had gotten a similar prognosis. It was awkward, she knew, to stand so close to death.

"It's fine, Fran," she said as she walked around her neighbor and set the mugs on the table.

Frances followed her, and then remained standing at the table as Margaret went back and got the coffeepot.

"So, tell me about your Christmas plans," Margaret said. She sat down at the table and then nodded toward Frances, inviting her to join her.

"I'll be with my son, Jimmy, and his wife. I think the three kids will come for part of the time. Jimmy wasn't sure. You know how teenagers are."

She smiled. “They finally bought their own place on the water in Boca Raton, in some fancy high-rise. We used to always rent something.”

Margaret nodded. She reached across her and took a packet of sugar from a small bowl in the center of the table. She put it in her coffee and stirred.

“I guess on Christmas Day, we’ll probably go out to dinner, maybe take a boat ride, if it’s nice.” Frances took a sip of her coffee and still fidgeted a bit in her seat.

Margaret pointed to the sugar and little pitcher of milk, and Frances shook her head. She liked her coffee black.

“A boat ride?” Margaret asked. “Does Jimmy have a boat down there too?”

Frances nodded. “One of those pontoon boats, party boats, they call them,” she explained.

Margaret nodded as if she understood. “Well, taking a boat ride for Christmas. That sounds unique, doesn’t it?”

Frances raised her eyebrows. “I know. I actually prefer snow and having a fire in the fireplace, drinking hot cider.” She paused. “But Florida is nice. I don’t have to pack much since you don’t need a coat or scarves or gloves.” She smiled.

“What about you, Margaret?” she asked. “Do you have special plans?” Then her face turned red as if she had asked something too personal. “I’m sorry,” she said quickly. She almost dropped her cup and spilled a bit on the table. Then she jumped up and hurried over to the sink to get a dishtowel to clean it. "I'm so sorry," she said again as she rushed back to the table.

Margaret stayed seated and tended to the spill.

"It's okay, Frances. Don't worry about it. I have some napkins right here," she said as she wiped up the coffee. "It's fine, sit down," she added. "I feel like you're hovering."

Frances sat down at the table. She was distraught.

"There's nothing wrong with you asking me about my holidays," Margaret said softly. "I have cancer but that doesn't mean I can't make plans for Christmas."

Tears welled in the other woman's eyes. "I just don't know what to say to you," she confessed. She dropped her face away from Margaret. She placed her hands in her lap. "I lied earlier. I wasn't too busy to visit. I stayed away on purpose because I don't know what to say. I'm just so sorry," she confessed.

Margaret smiled and nodded. "It's fine," she said reassuringly. "You're not the only one. It seems like folks find out that you're dying and they act like you're suddenly contagious or something."

"Oh no," Frances said, lifting her face and shaking her head, "I don't think that. That's not what I mean." She seemed more upset.

"It's okay, Fran," Margaret reached over and patted her neighbor on the hand and then took a sip from her coffee. “I know that this is hard for everybody else too.”

Frances nodded and sat back in her chair. She seemed to relax a bit now that she had made her confession. The two women sat in silence for a few minutes and Frances took a few deep breaths. She had resigned herself to staying.

“So, tell me, what do you like about Florida?” Margaret asked, trying to ease the tension that had arisen between the two old friends.

Frances seemed surprised by the question. She shrugged her shoulders and considered how to answer. “I don’t know. The truth is I don’t really like it,” she said. She reached out for her coffee cup again. She got the pot and poured another cup.

“I think going there in December just became a habit after Morris died,” she noted, referring to her husband who had passed away almost eight years before.

“Jimmy hated the thought of his mother being alone during the holidays and he didn’t want to come back here.” She drank some coffee. “He always wanted to be somewhere warm, so he was the one who started arranging this little trip.”

Margaret nodded. She remembered her neighbor’s son. He was grown when Frances and Morris moved in, but she had seen him visiting on a number of occasions.

“At first we would go for just a week and then it

became two weeks and now it’s the whole month.” She sighed.

“I think for the first couple of years I was so numb I would have gone along with any idea he suggested, and now, I guess, it’s just what we do. I don’t think too much about it anymore. I know it pleases Jimmy to have us together, and it’s nice to be with everybody.” She set her cup down. “I guess I just go because that’s what everybody expects. The truth is that I do it for him. I think it’s good for him.”

“I guess a mother’s job is never done, is it?” Margaret asked. She crossed her legs under the table. Her belly was hurting a little and she was trying to find a comfortable sitting position.

A car passed on the street in front of the house. Both women glanced out the window to see if anybody else was driving up the driveway. The two friends looked at each other and smiled.

“You didn’t lose much hair this time,” Frances noted. She seemed more like her old self now talking to Margaret.

“No, I don’t think I got enough of the chemicals in my system before they had to stop,” Margaret explained. “I’m glad not to have to take any more of those.” She ran her fingers through her short salt-and-pepper-colored hair. “And now I guess I’ll die with my own hair.”

Frances turned away. She took another sip of her coffee.

"Will you put up a tree?" Frances asked, trying to change the subject. She was more comfortable with her neighbor; but she did not want to talk about death, Margaret's or anybody else's.

Margaret seemed confused at first and then realized what her neighbor was asking. "Oh," she replied. "I think the girls are planning to bring one over this week," she replied. "Jessie and Lou and Bea," she added. "I heard them talking about it. I think they think I should have one."

And then Margaret considered her answer. "Well, there, you see, looks like we're doing our holidays the same way, aren't we? We're letting somebody else decide our celebration for us."

Frances nodded with a bit of uncertainty. She wasn't really following what Margaret was saying. "Don't you want a tree?" she asked.

Margaret took in a breath and thought about the question. "No, not really," she said, shaking her head. "I never liked cutting down a tree to put in my house for three weeks and then tossing it in the garbage. I always felt like I was killing something for my own pleasure. And I hate those artificial ones." Then she hesitated and turned back to her neighbor. "What about you?" she asked. "Do you have a tree in Florida?"

Frances scrunched up her face. "It's silver," she answered. "One of those fancy aluminum ones that sell for two hundred dollars, one of the kids bought it a couple of years ago. I never liked them."

"Do you want to go to Florida?"

Frances shook her head. "No," she replied honestly. "To be truthful, I'd rather stay here and decorate the house and go to the church pageant. I just love those. And I wish I could wear my favorite Christmas sweaters. I have four," she noted. "And I never get to wear them." She paused.

"And I like to bake, and Carolyn, that's Jimmy's wife," she said, as a side note to Margaret, "Carolyn doesn't have any cookware in the condo. She said Florida is for vacationing and vacationing is for eating out." Frances slumped a bit in her chair. She shrugged. "But in spite of that, I really love being with Jimmy and his kids. I love having family with me on Christmas Eve."

Margaret made a face at her neighbor. "So you go to Florida for the family, for Jimmy. There's nothing wrong with that. It sounds like something a good mother would do." She put her elbows on the table and leaned her face into her hands.

Frances considered what Margaret was getting at. The two women sat in silence for a while. They listened to the traffic and the sounds of the December morning.

"When I was real little my mother used to start making Christmas presents in the summer. She always wanted it to be special for all of us. She would knit scarves for her five children and make my sisters and me dolls and get our dad to carve my brothers little guns or whistles or something."

Margaret sat back in her chair. She hadn't thought of these things in years.

"For the longest time, I didn't know what she was doing in July and August. And when I asked her why she was knitting in the hot summer she'd always say, 'Oh, I'm thinking about Santa Claus and all that he has to do for next Christmas. I'm worried that he might need some help, and nobody helps Santa like a mother!' " Margaret smiled. "She never let us know how poor we were or what we didn't have. She only wanted the best for her children."

Frances blew out a breath and took her final sip of her coffee. "Yeah, my mother was like that too. She always tried to keep us from knowing how hard her life was or how much she was suffering. She would have done anything for us children, just to make sure that we were protected and safe. So I guess that's why instead of baking and decorating for Jimmy and the children, now I go on a boat ride and eat at a hotel buffet. But it doesn't really matter where we are or what we're doing, I love knowing that I'm helping make happy memories for Christmas."

Frances glanced over at Margaret and noticed that she had a strange look about her. "Are you okay?" she asked.

Margaret nodded and didn't explain the look or what she was feeling. "That's really lovely, Frances, what you do for Jimmy. You really are a good mother and a good friend."

And then she laughed slightly. "So maybe you could go fishing and cook up a marlin for Christmas in Boca Raton."

Frances smiled.

"Or maybe you could just take some of your own pots and pans and cook what you like for Jimmy and Carolyn and the kids."

"I guess," Frances responded, never having considered that as an option.

"Maybe they think you don't want to cook because they don't want to cook. But maybe if you told them you'd like to fix the meal, it would be nice for everybody."

Frances nodded.

"You could even turn up the air conditioning real high and wear your sweater!" Margaret smiled.

Frances looked at her neighbor. She could see how tired Margaret had gotten in just the short time they had visited. She knew she should probably leave. She considered that she ought to be relieved by that thought; but in actuality, it saddened her to say good-bye. "I should go," she said.

Margaret nodded. She was getting fatigued and sensed that she needed a little rest.

"What about you, Margaret?"

Margaret didn't understand the question.

"What do you want to do this Christmas?"

And even though she was tired and dying, Margaret was beginning to understand more clearly what it was she really wanted for that holiday.

# Section Three

❄❄❄

# Red Velvet Cake

❄❄❄

2 eggs
1½ cups sugar
1 cup oil
1 tablespoon vinegar
2 cups flour
1 teaspoon cocoa
1 teaspoon baking soda
1 teaspoon salt
1 cup buttermilk
2 teaspoons red food coloring

Beat eggs with sugar; add oil and vinegar. In a separate bowl, sift dry ingredients, add to egg mixture, alternating with buttermilk. Add red food coloring. Bake in 3 9-inch pans at 350 degrees for approximately 25 minutes. Frost cake with cream cheese filling.

# Chapter Eleven

"I'll just put the cake on the table." Louise walked into the house and right past Jessie and James as they sat in the den decorating the tree. She hadn't even bothered to knock.

"Okay," Jessie responded. It hadn't surprised her to have Louise walk in. She had told her to come by because she had needed to talk to her about something important.

"It's red velvet," Louise announced from the kitchen. "I hope you like it. This one is from Mary Jo Ledford," she added. She started taking out saucers and pulling out silverware. "I must have twenty cakes a day show up at my doorstep."

Jessie waited for her friend to come into the den to join her to hear more about the cake. Louise headed out of the kitchen and then over to the closet at the front door and removed her coat and gloves. She placed them in the closet and turned toward Jessie and James.

"You want me to start a pot of coffee?" Louise asked.

"There's some already made," Jessie replied.

Louise headed into the room where her friends were waiting.

"Ever since the word got out that Beatrice had arranged for the winner of our contest to meet the

Cake Lady, everybody's sending me recipes and showing up at my house with cakes." Louise walked into the room rubbing her belly. "Let me just say that I have had the opportunity to enjoy a vast assortment of Christmas cakes."

"Lou, just because they're bringing them to you doesn't mean that you have to sample them all!" Jessie noted.

Louise smiled. "I know it." She sat down on the sofa across from Jessie. "But I've discovered I have a kind of weakness about cakes. And besides, if I'm going to be bribed, I might as well enjoy it!"

"So maybe Beatrice's claim has had a few benefits," Jessie said.

"Well, if you mean these extra ten pounds, I'd say so!"

"Has she secured a prize yet?" Jessie asked.

Louise shook her head. Then she walked over to the tree to help James untangle the strands of light. "She still swears that she can get the Cake Lady."

Jessie shook her head.

"She just won't give it up," Louise said. "She just won't admit that she's made a mistake and let me tell everybody that this crazy story that she concocted is not true. Imagine, some television star coming to Hope Springs and judging this silly cake contest."

"She wouldn't go for the cash prize from the church?" Jessie asked.

"Are you kidding?" Louise responded. "She said

that she could never let the winner receive money for her contest."

"Let me guess," Jessie interrupted, "because it looks bad for a church?"

"You got it," Louise replied. "Then she went on about the Episcopalians and how they give out money for everything."

"What is it with her and those Episcopalians?" Jessie asked. She was opening another box.

"I couldn't tell you," Louise said.

"Haven't you already taken the cookbook to the printer?" Jessie wanted to know. She started taking out ornaments, unwrapping them out of the tissue paper, and setting them on the coffee table.

"We'll have them back by the weekend, which is great. Folks can still buy them before Christmas next week. It's just that we don't have a winner to post inside the book. But I just thought we should go ahead and get the books done. I couldn't wait any longer on Beatrice."

"Well, I guess they can be considered as separate, the contest and the cookbook, I mean." Jessie found the box of hooks and started putting them on top of the ornaments for hanging.

"James, did you tie these lights together last year?" Louise asked.

He smiled. "I believe that was somebody else's doing," he replied.

Jessie let out a laugh. She remembered that she

had taken down the lights the previous Christmas and she remembered how aggravated her husband had been when he got home and saw the mess she had made.

They pulled and untangled. There were several strands all wrapped together.

"So, what is the news?" Louise asked as she worked on the lights.

"It's Margaret," Jessie said. "She's told me something and I'm not sure what she wants me to do with the information."

Louise finally found an end and was able to loosen a knot. She handed what she had untangled to James, who began hanging the strand on the tree.

"She said that there's something missing in her life."

Louise waited for more.

"It has something to do with her mother and her mother's home place. She was from Texas." Jessie sat in the rocking chair, going through the box of Christmas decorations.

Louise was able to keep untangling the strands and James kept wrapping the lights around the tree.

"I never heard her mention her mother," Louise noted. She was very surprised when Jessie had called her to the house to talk about Margaret.

"I never knew her to talk about her either," Jessie explained. "She died when Margaret was only a little girl. She went back to Texas to have her mother and sisters take care of her and she died in her home."

"In Texas?" Louise asked, reaching around the tree and helping James attach the lights to the branches.

Jessie nodded her head. "Goodlett is the name of the town." She had most of the ornaments out and on the coffee table. "Margaret said that she only went there once, the Christmas before her mother died. And that she regretted that she never went back."

"I didn't know," Louise said.

Louise and James finished with the lights. She stood back as James plugged them in. They all held their breath and waited. Suddenly the tree was lit up and they all applauded. Louise walked back over to the sofa.

"Well, at least they work," Jessie commented, and gave a big smile to her husband.

"This year, I take down the tree," James announced.

"Fine with me," his wife agreed. And then she whispered over to Louise, "That was my plan all along."

Louise smiled.

"I heard that," James said from across the room.

"What is this?" Louise asked as she pulled out an ornament and showed it to Jessie. It was tangled in wrapping paper and looked like what used to be an angel. It had been made of wax and it had melted, creating an unusual shape.

"Oh, Mrs. Howard!" Jessie exclaimed and reached over, taking the ornament. She made a kind of clucking noise with her tongue. "I think Wallace made her in kindergarten." She tried to fix the misshapen piece. "We've had her a long time," she lamented.

"Why did you name her Mrs. Howard?" Louise wanted to know. She took the ornament from Jessie to examine it.

"Oh, I don't know. That was something Wallace decided." Jessie shook her head. "He had it in his mind that God's name was Howard and since he made this angel to be a woman, he decided that it was God's wife and her name was Mrs. Howard."

Louise looked confused. "Jessie, why did your grandson think God's name was Howard?"

"Because of the prayer," James answered for his wife. He was still standing behind the tree, trying to attach a timer to the extension cord and the outlet.

Louise handed the ornament back to Jessie, still wanting to hear more.

" 'Our Father, who art in heaven, Hallowed be thy name . . .' " He added, "He thought it was 'Howard be thy name.' Hence, Mrs. Howard was the angel's name." He glanced around the tree and winked over in Jessie's direction. He recalled when his grandson had told him that story.

Louise laughed. "Well, Mrs. Howard looks like she may have played too close to the devil. She's got some pretty serious burns!"

Jessie nodded. "I know." She studied the small ornament that Louise handed to her. "Maybe we could melt her a bit and reshape her."

"Maybe you just need to let her go," Louise suggested. She started pulling out a few more ornaments.

"Oh, I hate to throw away God's wife," Jessie said. "I'll just put her over here and let Wallace decide what to do with her." She placed the angel on the coffee table and took another one of the ornaments from Louise.

"James, honey, look at this one." Jessie held up an ornament. It was old and made from tin.

He glanced from around the tree. When he saw what his wife was holding, he smiled. "Ah, it's your granddaddy's," he said.

"What is it?" Louise asked. She looked closely at the ornament in Jessie's hand but was unable to decipher the shape of the antique.

Jessie smiled. "It's a train," she said as she studied it.

"And it was your grandfather's?" Louise asked.

"Yep," Jessie replied. "My father bought it for his father."

"Really?" Louise asked. "Did he like trains?"

"No, it was more of a promise," she replied, taking the ornament to the tree and hanging it.

Then she continued. “He left his parents down south, Mississippi,” she clarified. “And he promised them that he would bring them up here to North Carolina when he got settled.”

James moved back behind the tree. He was going to let his wife tell the story.

“So, what happened?” Louise asked.

Jessie went back to her seat. “They died before he ever saved up enough to get them here.” She shook her head. “He never forgave himself for that, for not keeping his promise.”

The three were silent for a while. Finally James walked around to where more boxes had been placed and picked up one from the top. “Do you want me to take these kitchen things out?”

“Sure, baby. Just put them in there on the table. I think it’s mostly just a few dishtowels, maybe some coffee mugs.”

He nodded and headed into the kitchen with the box.

“Okay, back to Margaret,” Louise shifted the conversation. “Why do you think that she mentioned her mother and her mother’s hometown?” she asked.

Jessie smiled and nodded her head. She was glad to change the subject. “She said that Frances Martin came over and that they started talking about Christmas plans and that Frances goes to Florida.”

“Boca Raton,” Louise noted.

"Right, Boca Raton," Jessie agreed. "Does Jimmy have a house there?" she asked.

"A condo, I think," Louise replied. "He lives in South Carolina, doesn't he?"

Jessie nodded. They both paused for a minute, recalling the young man whose mother lived next door to Margaret.

"Anyway, they were having this conversation and Margaret said that she realized that the one thing that she's never done is to see her people again, go back to Goodlett, Texas."

"Was there some reason that she brought this up?" Louise asked.

Jessie shrugged. "I never heard her talk about wanting to visit out there. Have you?"

"No," Louise noted. She thought about the idea. "I did know that she talked about visiting Texas if she ever went to see Charlotte. Do you think that's what this is about? Do you think she wants us to get Charlotte here to see her?"

Jessie shrugged again.

"Where exactly is this place?" Louise wanted to know.

"Somewhere near Amarillo. She said it was a few hours from Oklahoma City, off of Interstate 40. She said it wasn't far from the Oklahoma border."

"I don't know anything about that part of the country," Louise said.

"Me neither," Jessie responded.

The two women got up from their seats and started hanging the ornaments on the tree. There was no conversation for a few minutes.

"Are we putting up a tree at Margaret's this weekend like we planned?" Louise asked.

Jessie shrugged her shoulders. "That was why I was over there in the first place, to ask her if she wanted me to bring her decorations down from the attic. She said that she didn't want to decorate her house this year." She held up three matching red and green knitted stockings and hung them from the branches.

"Do you think she's depressed?" Louise asked.

Jessie sighed. The thought had certainly crossed her mind. "Wouldn't you be?" she asked.

Louise thought about that. She nodded slowly as she walked over to the coffee table and got some more ornaments to hang. The two women decorated without saying anything else. They considered their friend and whether they should force decorations upon her. They weren't sure what they needed to do for Margaret for Christmas.

Finally they heard a voice coming from the kitchen. "You take her to Texas." It was James.

"What?" Jessie asked.

"You take her to her mamma's place," James said as he walked into the room where the two women stood.

"We've never been to that place. And it's winter.

You can't take off west. The weather is too unpredictable," Louise responded.

"Then you prepare for the weather," James announced. He stood behind the rocking chair where his wife had been sitting. "She told you about this place and this regret because she wants you to take her there."

Louise and Jessie both stared at James in amazement. They couldn't believe that he was making a suggestion like that.

"James, it's a week before Christmas. That has to be a two- or three-day trip, at least. We don't even know if she's up for a drive that far. And then we don't even know where she's talking about. How would we make a trip like that?" she asked.

"I'm just telling you what you need to do for your friend." He looked over at the tree. His stare was focused on the old train ornament he had just hung. "She told you about this because she's hoping that you'll make a way for her to do this last thing that she wants to do."

"How do you know this, James?" Louise asked.

He shook his head. "I don't know about Margaret and what kinds of questions she's asking at this point in her life. I don't know what she thinks about what the doctors have said and whether she knows this is her last Christmas or not." He looked over at his wife. "But I do know about dreams. And I know about regret. I had a few of my own and you fixed that, Jessie. You let me come back home so that I didn't have to die with mine."

Jessie studied her husband, remembering how he left for so long and then how it was when he came back. She thought about her father and how he regretted never getting his parents out of Mississippi.

"Margaret shouldn't die with regret."

Louise and Jessie turned to each other.

"She doesn't want any tree or fancy decorations at her house. She wants to go to this place she remembers from her childhood. She wants to see the place and remember how it felt to be young." James straightened up and folded his arms around his chest. "And you two and crazy Bea are the only ones who can give her that. So, that's what you've got to do."

Jessie looked at her husband and her eyes filled with tears. "No regrets," she said.

They nodded at each other.

"Well, Louise, I guess we better start making some travel arrangements."

And Louise hung the last angel on the tree and rubbed her hands together as if she was just getting started with a new project.

# Old-Fashioned Yellow Cake with Caramel Icing

1 cup shortening
2 cups sugar
4 eggs
2¼ teaspoons baking powder
¾ teaspoon salt
3 cups flour
1 cup milk
1 teaspoon vanilla

Cream shortening and sugar. Add eggs one at a time, beating well after each addition. Add baking powder and salt to flour. Start adding flour to shortening mixture and alternate with milk, ending up with flour. Add vanilla. Bake at 375 degrees in 3 9-inch pans for 20 minutes.

[*continued*]

## CARAMEL ICING

½ cup butter
1 cup brown sugar
¼ cup milk
1¾ or 2 cups powdered sugar

Melt butter; add sugar and boil over low heat for 2 minutes. Add milk and stir until mixture comes to a boil. Remove from heat and cool. Beat in powdered sugar. Spread between layers and cover top and sides.

# Chapter Twelve

"Near Amarillo?" Charlotte was on the phone with Jessie. She was trying to finish up the end-of-the-year figures for the upcoming board of directors meeting and still putting the final touches on the Christmas party she was planning for the women at the shelter. It was a busy day.

"I never heard Margaret say that she was from Texas," she said.

"It's not Margaret who is from Texas, it was her mother," Jessie responded. "Her mother's people are from there."

"I thought everybody in her family was from North Carolina?"

"On her daddy's side I think that's right. But her mother's people were ranchers in west Texas."

"Didn't her mother die when she was a little girl?" Charlotte asked.

"Ten," Jessie replied. "She died when Margaret was ten."

Charlotte thought about what Jessie was suggesting, trying to recall if Margaret had ever spoken about her mother, about visiting Texas. She couldn't remember any conversation. She knew that Margaret's father raised her and that she spent a lot of time outside on the farm, but the young minister had never thought to ask her about her mother and what had happened or where she was from.

"And she wants to go there?" Charlotte asked, sounding surprised. "And now?" She shook her head. She didn't understand what her friend needed.

"I think it's something she's wanted for some time but never asked anybody to take her or go with her."

"Does she still have family there?" Charlotte wanted to know.

Jessie thought about this question. She and Louise had discussed this as well. She had even asked Margaret the very same thing. "She doesn't think so. Distant cousins, maybe, but there's no one she recalls or even wants to see."

"Then what is this about?" Charlotte had lots of questions since this didn't seem like Margaret at all. She had never known her friend to want to take a trip on such short notice. In fact, except for a cruise that Margaret mentioned taking after her husband died, she didn't recall Margaret ever talking about taking any trip or vacation.

"She hasn't really said," Jessie responded. "She just wants to go."

"It's only a week before Christmas," Charlotte said.

"I know," Jessie said. "Will it be a hardship for you to take off and meet us there?" she asked. "I just think it would mean a lot for her to have you there too."

Charlotte didn't hesitate. "Of course I will be there. Do you know when you might arrive?"

Jessie waited before answering. She hadn't considered all the arrangements that she was going to have to make. "Well, if we can leave over the weekend, we should be able to get to Goodlett by the twenty-third. Beatrice is getting us a van and Louise is trying to make hotel reservations. I'm calling you and supposed to talk to the doctor and make sure of everything we might need if she gets sick. At this point, he didn't seem to think it would be a problem."

Charlotte didn't respond. She was thinking about everything Jessie was saying. "Did Margaret ask you about this?" she asked.

"No," Jessie replied. "Not at first. At first it was James's idea."

"James?" Charlotte asked. "Why did James know what Margaret wanted?"

"He just guessed. Margaret had told me about Goodlett and wanting to visit and never getting there. She said something about her mother and Christmas and how it had been the most wonderful Christmas she had ever had but she didn't say she wanted to go. But surprise of surprises, he was right. When I brought it up to Margaret, she cried. And she said it was exactly the thing she wanted for Christmas."

"That's amazing that he could figure that out," Charlotte said.

"Yep, he has a gift."

"So, you get to Goodlett, Texas, and then what?" Charlotte wanted to know.

"Well, that part is up to Margaret." Jessie paused. "She wants to go to some church and she wants to go to her mother's grave."

Charlotte nodded. Now it was starting to make sense. "She's going to make some peace, isn't she?"

"Looks that way," Jessie replied.

"Well." Charlotte was considering what she needed to do to make the trip to meet her friends. "I will need to get some things taken care of here but I should be able to meet you by Tuesday. It probably won't take me a couple of days to drive there."

She pulled out the road atlas she kept on a shelf behind her desk. She opened it to Texas and starting looking for the place Jessie had mentioned. "As soon as I can find Goodlett . . . where is it again?" she asked.

"Go across Oklahoma on Interstate 40," Jessie instructed. She was studying her map too.

"Okay, I got that," Charlotte responded.

"Now, just as you cross the border, drop down, going south on Highway 83."

"To Childress?" Charlotte asked.

"Right," Jessie said. "Then take Highway 287 east." She waited for a second. "Do you see it?" she asked.

"No," Charlotte answered. "It isn't on this map." She shook her head. "How far does it look to be from Childress?"

"Ten or fifteen miles, maybe," Jessie noted.

"I'll find it, I'm sure. And there probably aren't too many cemeteries in that little town too. We'll find each other. Do you have my cell phone number?" Charlotte asked.

"Yes," Jessie replied. "We'll touch base along the way, okay?"

"Perfect," Charlotte said as she closed the map. "Do you think we can find a place there we can stay?"

"Well, I suppose if not, we'll get back on the interstate until we find something. Maybe we can look in Childress if there isn't anything in her hometown."

Charlotte thought about hotels and wondered if she could check on the computer to find a place for them to stay. She decided that she could think about that later. She closed the map. Then she needed to ask the question she had been putting off. "She's nearing the end, isn't she?"

Jessie waited. She knew how hard it was for Charlotte to think about losing Margaret. "I think so," she finally responded.

There was a pause between the two friends.

"I don't know exactly what this trip is about but I have some idea it's something she needs to do before she can die," Jessie remarked.

"In peace," Charlotte added.

"In peace," Jessie repeated.

"I remember one time that she told me that peace was the one spiritual gift she felt had eluded her all of her life. She said that she felt as if her entire life had something blocking that from her and she never quite understood what it was."

Jessie considered what Charlotte was telling her. She had always thought of Margaret as a peaceful person, but she realized then that based upon what Charlotte was saying, Margaret had apparently never completely felt that way. It saddened her a bit to think her best friend had never known that sense of contentment.

"Well, I guess she's figured it out now," Jessie said. "And that's always a good thing, isn't it?"

"And it's in Texas," Charlotte noted with a smile.

"Goodlett, a place that isn't even on the maps. And we'll find it for her on Christmas."

Charlotte laughed a bit. "I have thought of a lot of places I would like to go for Christmas. I thought of Europe and Costa Rica, but I have to confess, I have never thought of Goodlett, Texas."

"Who knew?" Jessie said.

The two women thought about what they were planning and chuckled a bit more.

"Okay, I'll call you when we're ready to leave, and maybe by then I'll have a little more information about where we're staying and how long it will take us to get there."

"That's fine," Charlotte said. "I'll see if I can find anywhere for us to stay while we're there and I will plan to meet you somewhere in Goodlett, Texas, next week." She paused. "Thank you, Jessie, for doing this for Margaret, for doing this for me."

"That's what friends are for," Jessie replied. "And I figured you would want to be there."

"You figured right," Charlotte said.

"Then we'll see you soon."

"Okay, good-bye, Jessie."

"Good-bye, Charlotte."

When Charlotte glanced up as she was putting the receiver back on the phone base, she noticed that the shelter's newest client, Rachel, was standing in her doorway. Charlotte could see how much better she was doing, how her bruises were healing, how much better she was walking now, without the use of crutches.

"You need some help with the party?" she asked.

"Oh, sure, that would be great," Charlotte replied. "We need some snacks and desserts. Do you cook?"

"I can bake a plain cake and I can make a real nice icing. My grandmother taught me."

Charlotte smiled.

"It's caramel," Rachel noted. "Is that okay for Christmas?"

"Of course," Charlotte replied.

The young woman stayed standing at the door.

Charlotte could tell that she wanted to say something else. Charlotte waited.

Rachel glanced around the office and then asked, "You going to Texas?"

Charlotte smiled. She wondered if the young woman had been listening to her conversation with Jessie. "Yeah," she replied. "A friend of mine wants to see her family," she added.

"Where she from?" Rachel asked.

Charlotte could hear the Texan accent more clearly now. She realized that she liked it. She didn't hear it too much, and the Southern drawl made her a bit homesick for her family and friends.

"Goodlett," Charlotte replied. "You know of it?" She remembered that Rachel was from Childress, the town that Jessie had used as a reference point.

"Sure, I heard of Goodlett," Rachel responded. She leaned against the door frame. "Not much there," she noted.

"Yeah, I guess not. I can't even find it on my map," Charlotte explained.

Rachel smiled. "It's fourteen miles south of where I grew up," she said. "I used to go with a boy from Goodlett."

"Oh," Charlotte was intrigued. This was the most information that her new client had shared since arriving at the shelter more than a month earlier.

"You from Texas?" Rachel asked Charlotte.

"No, North Carolina," she replied. "You hear my Southern flavor?" she asked.

Rachel smiled. “I knew you weren’t from here.”

“How did you know that?” Charlotte asked.

Rachel shrugged. “Just the way you talk. It’s slow.” She paused. “I like it,” she added.

Charlotte smiled. “I was thinking the same thing about the way you talked. I’m glad to hear more of it today.” She opened the map back up to find out where fourteen miles south of Childress took her. She slid her finger down the highway line and stopped. There was in fact a tiny name written just where Jessie had said. She had simply missed it.

“You spend a lot of time with this boyfriend from Goodlett?” Charlotte asked. She was thinking about how long the trip would take her from Gallup.

“Not so much really. He was nice. I was just looking for my way out of Childress. Goodlett wasn’t far enough away for me.”

Charlotte nodded.

“His daddy bought a cotton gin there,” she explained. “But I think he was going to turn it into a trailer park.”

“Hmmm. That sounds nice.” Charlotte didn’t quite know what to say. “My friend Margaret,” she said, “her mother was from there but she’s been dead a long time.”

Rachel nodded. “She wanting to visit the grave?” she asked.

“I think so,” Charlotte said. She hesitated. “She’s sick,” she added. “I think she wants to go and see her mother before she dies.”

Rachel nodded again. “I understand that,” she said. “I used to go down to my grandmother’s grave every day. I talked to her. I bought her new flowers every week but I went to see her every day. She was the only one I was ever able to talk to.”

“How old were you when she died?” Charlotte asked.

“Fourteen,” Rachel answered. “She raised me. She and my uncle Nestor.”

The young woman walked into the office.

Charlotte gestured for her to sit down in the chair across from her desk. She was glad that Rachel was opening up. “I guess you miss her,” Charlotte surmised.

“Yep,” Rachel responded.

And then Charlotte had an interesting idea. She sat up a bit in her chair. “You want to go with me?” she asked.

Rachel stared at Charlotte. “To Childress?” she asked.

Charlotte shrugged.

“I never thought about going back,” Rachel responded. “I just thought I never could go back once I left.”

“Why would you think that?” Charlotte asked, surprised at Rachel’s comment. “Why would you think you could never go back?”

“I just thought I had made such a mess of things that nobody would want me back.”

“Your uncle still there?” Charlotte asked.

Rachel nodded. "And my sister." She hesitated. "She's older than me, just a couple of years, but we haven't spoken to each other in a long time."

"Why?" Charlotte asked. She was glad to have her newest client talking so much, and since she didn't know if Rachel would ever open up again like this, she thought she would keep asking her questions.

Rachel shrugged. "I'm not sure now," she replied honestly. "Rainey was sixteen and she wanted to get out of town more than me, so she left. After that, when she called I wouldn't talk to her because it made me so mad that she left me." The young woman folded her arms across her chest.

"You ever see her again?" Charlotte asked.

Rachel nodded her head. "Once," she answered.

Charlotte waited for the explanation.

"She came back to town before I left with Roy, tried to get me not to go." She fidgeted a bit in her seat.

"Is Roy the boy who beat you up?" Charlotte asked.

Rachel nodded. "Rainey knew about him. She knew he would kill me, so when she heard that I had took up with him, she came back to try and get me not to leave with him."

Charlotte slid her elbows on the desk and leaned her face into her hands. She was glad to hear Rachel talking so much. It surprised her because the young woman had been silent for so long.

"But you went anyway?" Charlotte asked.

Rachel grinned. Her front tooth was still broken where Roy had hit her in the face with a baseball bat. "I'm kind of hardheaded," she confessed.

Charlotte smiled.

"So, your sister is the one back in Texas and you're the one who left?" she asked.

Rachel shrugged. "I guess," she replied.

"Don't you want to see her?"

She gave another shrug. "I don't know," she replied. "I guess I never thought about it."

"Well, I'm leaving next week for a town fourteen miles south of Childress to see a friend of mine who is dying. You are welcome to ride along with me and I will drop you off in your grandmother's town and pick you up on my way back, or you can go with me to Goodlett and see your old boyfriend."

Rachel smiled. "I might just think about it," she replied.

"Good enough." And the phone rang, pulling Charlotte back into the job and the multiple tasks at hand. "Tell Tempest what you need for the cake and she can pick the stuff up at the grocery store when she goes."

"Okay," Rachel responded. And for the first time, she actually seemed at ease with herself and the place where she had landed.

# Lemon Lavender Pound Cake

❄❄❄

3 cups flour
½ teaspoon salt
½ teaspoon baking powder
½ pound butter
½ cup vegetable shortening
3 cups sugar
5 large eggs
1 cup milk
1 teaspoon lavender
1 teaspoon lemon extract

Sift flour, salt, and baking powder together. Cream butter and vegetable shortening thoroughly. Add sugar a little at a time, creaming well after each addition. Add eggs one at a time, beating well after each egg. Add sifted flour mixture and milk alternately, beginning and ending with flour. Add lavender and lemon flavorings. Bake in a tube pan at 325 degrees for 1 hour and 20 minutes or until done.

# Chapter Thirteen

"Tell her it's Beatrice Witherspoon from Hope Springs, North Carolina," Beatrice was trying again to reach the famous Cake Lady by phone. Since the first phone call when she talked to some assistant, she hadn't been able to get past this person she assumed was the receptionist at the studio.

"Do you know if she's gotten my letters?" Beatrice asked, sounding a bit helpless. "Well, do you know if she's made a decision about the contest?"

The woman on the other end was of no help at all to Beatrice.

"No, I don't want to leave a message. I've left a hundred messages and no one will call me back." She blew out a breath and hung up the phone.

She didn't know how she was going to follow through on her promise to have the Cake Lady serve as the judge for the contest. Here it was only a few days before Christmas, the cake cookbooks had been printed and were "out on the market," as Louise said; and her phone, when she wasn't trying to reach the woman in New York, was ringing off the hook with people wanting to know which cake was the winning recipe.

She had even gotten a call from the prison. That

hadn't happened in a long time, not since she stopped writing a few of the inmates. It seemed that one of the men had heard about the contest and sent Louise a recipe. Beatrice had found it in the cookbook. It was for Lemon Lavender Pound Cake and it actually sounded pretty tasty. But now he was calling Beatrice as well. He wanted to know, if he won, whether he would need to arrange a work release permit to bake his cake on the television show.

This whole thing was turning out to be a huge mess and Beatrice knew it. She sat by the phone as it rang and chose not to answer it. She couldn't take being asked the same question one more time.

She knew she should have listened to her husband and even Louise. She should have simply admitted that she made a mistake and that the Cake Lady wasn't going to judge the contest, and made arrangements for some other kind of prize, a kind of prize that she could manage.

Beatrice could have managed a small cash prize; even the pastor of the church had said there was a little money left over in the miscellaneous budget. She knew she could have gotten an article in the Greensboro paper. She could have managed getting the cake featured in the local bakery or served at the church Christmas pageant. At the very least, she could have put the recipe and the winner in the church newsletter. She could have found some suitable prize that would have been acceptable to all those who entered a recipe in the contest.

She should have just admitted that she couldn't get the Cake Lady and moved on. She could have said that the Cake Lady changed her mind or that it was just too difficult to talk to such a big star. If she had done that, she would be finished with the project by now, able to sit back and enjoy Christmas, instead of having her phone constantly ringing with poor, desperate people looking for their fifteen minutes of fame.

She wouldn't have to run from people in stores and avoid those women at church wanting to know when the Cake Lady was going to name the winner. And she wouldn't have to worry about seeing Betty Mills at the funeral home Christmas party.

Beatrice knew that Betty would gloat when she found out that the Cake Lady wasn't participating. She knew that her husband's first cousin's wife would be pleased as punch to know that Beatrice Newgarden Witherspoon had to eat her words, go back on a promise, not be able to deliver up what she had promised. Beatrice knew that Betty had been waiting for such an opportunity ever since Bea had married into the family. The truth was that she knew that Betty had never liked her and had never thought she was good enough for Dick.

The ringing stopped and Beatrice gave a sigh of relief. At least she was spared one more query. At least she wouldn't have to put off what she knew was bound to happen soon enough. She didn't have to say that the Cake Lady was a no-show and that there was no prize for the contest.

She glanced across the room at her Christmas tree. She and Dick had put it up a couple of weeks before, and when they had done so, it had been a lovely evening for the two of them. The hormones had kicked in by then and she was feeling cheerful and eager to decorate.

The two of them had laughed and listened to carols and even had little glasses of sherry. It had been the nicest time they had shared in many months. She was glad to be feeling back to herself and she was grateful for her husband and for her friends for helping her get her back on track. If she had known that a patch on her butt could have made her feel this good, this levelheaded, she would have stuck one on there years ago. She smiled to herself with that thought.

And then Beatrice thought about Margaret. She wished there was a patch to stick on her butt to help with her grief or a patch that could wipe away Margaret's cancer. That would be something to celebrate. She closed her eyes. She could hardly let herself imagine what was happening with Margaret, what the future more than likely held for her.

She wondered if it was true what Jessie had said to her yesterday, that this was her friend's last

Christmas. She wondered how it was for Margaret, how she was feeling, if she knew that this was her last Christmas. Beatrice thought about herself and wondered how she would feel if she thought that this would be her last holiday celebration, her last tree, her last occasion to sing the songs she loved, "Silent Night" and "Joy to the World," all those carols she and Dick had only recently sung through the night.

Beatrice thought again of Margaret and how she was dealing with her circumstances, what she would say to Beatrice if she heard her complaining about the mess she had made. She knew Margaret would simply say that Beatrice was crazy for worrying about what people thought of her for making a mistake or promising something she couldn't deliver. She knew that no-nonsense Margaret would tell her that what Betty Mills thought of her was insignificant and that Beatrice should just shake it off and move on. Margaret never worried about what others thought about her and she never worried about saying she was wrong or had made a mistake. In her entire life, she had never seemed anxious about the small things.

After all, it had always been Margaret who had said, "Life is too short for this silliness." And that had been years before she had gotten sick, years before the cancer and now this recurrence. Margaret had always had a way of approaching life that was unsullied and clear. She was someone who always knew what had to be done and just did it. She was unwavering and coolheaded in all her life's decisions, all her life's dealings. So it didn't really surprise Beatrice that Margaret would be handling her death in the same sort of clear, precise way.

There had been no outbursts of self-pity, no momentary lapses of faith. Margaret had heard the prognosis, tried the treatments, then denied them, and was facing the inevitable outcome like some super person, some saint. In truth, that was why this idea to go to Texas surprised Beatrice. It was not like Margaret to become sentimental in this way, to have a need to make something right with a ghost, even if the ghost was her mother. It just didn't seem like something Margaret would need to do on her last Christmas.

Beatrice, however, had no intention of blocking this idea. She certainly was not the one to question this crazy whim of the cookbook committee members. In fact, with her circumstances as they were, getting out of town sounded like a perfect solution. She just wasn't sure what Margaret was thinking, and she was worried that Margaret might not find what she was searching for. And the disappointment that might follow worried Beatrice. She was concerned about the trip to Texas, to Margaret's mother's hometown, because she was worried that whatever Margaret needed, she wouldn't get.

Beatrice opened her eyes when she heard the knock on the door. She thought about not answering it, worried that it was someone else from the church trying to find out about the contest. And then she heard Louise's voice. It had become very familiar after she and Jessie had dropped by with their intervention.

"Beatrice, it's Louise, open the door."

Beatrice got up from her chair and went over to the door. "Hey," she said to her friend.

"Hey nothing. Where have you been?" she asked as she walked in the room.

"Nowhere," Beatrice replied. She shut the door behind Louise.

"I have been trying to call you. Are you not answering your phone? Are you taking your hormones?"

"Oh, um . . ." She tried to think of an excuse. "No, I still have the patch, want to see?" And she turned around and lifted up her blouse. She started to pull down her pants.

"Never mind." Louise waved off the answer and turned aside. "Jessie says we're leaving today. There's a winter storm supposed to hit Texas by Christmas Day; so we're moving out this afternoon."

Beatrice looked stunned.

"You did find us a van, didn't you?" Louise asked.

"Of course," Beatrice replied, trying to sound assured.

The truth was, with all of the decorating and worrying about the contest, she had forgotten her one assignment for the trip. She was supposed to call the rental agencies and reserve a van.

"Well, do you think you can get it today instead of tomorrow?" Louise asked. "What's this?" she asked, glancing over at a cookie tin.

"Brownies," Beatrice replied. "Here, have one." And she opened the tin and moved it closer to where Louise was standing.

"No." She shook her head and raised her hand toward Beatrice. "I've had so much cake I could go all next year without anything else sweet." She made a face and then thought about it. "What kind of brownies?" she asked.

"Blond ones, with chocolate chips and coconut," Beatrice replied.

Louise shook her head. "No, that's all right."

"Oh, okay," Beatrice responded, and pulled the tin over to her and put the top back in place.

"So, pick up the van this morning and come over and get me and then we will get Jessie and finally Margaret." She patted Beatrice on the hand. "Thanks for taking care of this part. I've arranged us a place to stay in Knoxville and then in Little Rock, Arkansas. After that, we'll just have to figure out where to go next."

Beatrice nodded. "You think we can be in Knoxville by tonight?" she asked, trying to think about how long of a drive that was.

"Well, I figure that it will be late, but it will depend upon what time we are able to leave this afternoon. How long will it take you to get ready?" Louise asked.

Beatrice shrugged. "I don't know. A couple of hours, I guess." She thought about the new change in plans. She had not checked about renting a van. She suddenly became concerned she would not be able to find one. Renting a vehicle was going to take her a little bit of time. She glanced at the clock.

"How long should I reserve the van for?" she asked, shrugging off her concerns.

Louise considered the question. "Well, if it takes us three days to get there and then we stay a day, that takes us to the twenty-third. After that, I guess Margaret will decide about whether she wants to stay for Christmas or not." She turned to Beatrice. "This okay with Dick?" she asked.

Beatrice nodded. "Yea, he's working anyway and the girls were all here at Thanksgiving so we weren't going to see them until January. And Teddy, well, he's still studying in South America somewhere."

Louise smiled. She was glad that all the women were able to work out holiday plans to make this trip with Margaret.

"Once we get to Knoxville, then how far is it to Little Rock?" Beatrice hadn't had a chance to study a map.

“It’s about five hundred and thirty miles,” Louise responded.

“So, that shouldn’t cause for a heavy travel day on Sunday, right?”

“Right,” Louise replied. “Okay, so, you’ll get the van and come to get me. What do you think, about one o’clock?” she asked. She was looking at the clock on the kitchen wall. She thought that allowing four hours was plenty for them all to get ready and for Beatrice to pick up the van. She assumed they had the one reserved for tomorrow already on the lot. She was going to ask Beatrice where she had called to make the reservation but then she noticed how her friend was staring at her.

“What?” Louise asked, sensing that something wasn’t right about the look she was getting.

“Do you pray?” Beatrice asked.

“What?” Louise was surprised by the question, especially since there were so many things that had to be done before they left in a few hours.

“Do you pray? About Margaret, I mean,” Beatrice explained. “I think about her all the time, but I don’t know how to pray about it.”

Louise, who had been standing the entire time, finally sat down on the stool at the bar. Beatrice thought she was going to yell at her for bringing up the subject so she stood very still, waiting for the onslaught.

“Every second, every minute, every day, I’m

praying," Louise replied. "I pray for a miracle and for her physical healing. I pray that she'll go back to the doctors after Christmas and discover that the cancer is gone. I promise God that if that happens I will become a television preacher and do whatever he asks." She slumped against the counter. "I pray that he take me instead, move the tumors, the irregular cells, the cancer over into my body and let her live."

She stopped and turned to Beatrice. "It's Christmas, right, so why can't we have a miracle in Hope Springs? Why can't we have Margaret healed of this crazy disease and let our lives go back to normal?"

Beatrice nodded. She was glad for Louise's candidness because she had thought and wondered the same things. She also knew that Louise was probably taking the news about Margaret harder than anyone else, and she was curious about how Louise was really doing.

"So I'll keep praying for the miracle, this Christmas miracle. I'm going to plead and beg for God to give her another shot. And I'm going to get in a van and drive with my three best friends to a place I've never been before, to some little hick town in Texas, and I'm going to do whatever Margaret wants to do."

"But maybe the healing isn't about the physical body, Lou. Maybe the healing has to do with her spirit, with her soul. Just because a person gets healed doesn't mean that they live forever. We all have to die, right?"

"That's a lovely little sermon, Beatrice. I'm so glad a patch on your butt has given you such theological expertise. But I don't care about any other healing for Margaret. I want her around. I want her to decide to take the chemotherapy again and I want her to fight and I want her to stay here for me." Louise rubbed her eyes. She was tired from everything.

"That's why you're going to Texas?" Beatrice asked, surprised at what Louise was saying.

"Yes, I would say so," she replied.

"You think that if she goes to her mother's grave that maybe she'll change her mind and go back into treatments?" Beatrice had no idea this was the way Louise was considering the trip they were taking together.

"Yes," Louise replied. "I'm hoping that Margaret will think about her mother's death and how early it came and decide that she has lived a lot longer and that she can live even longer if she fights. I'm thinking that a good sit at her mother's grave will give her the resolve to come home and keep fighting."

"She's fought a lot, Lou," Beatrice responded.

"I don't care," Louise confessed. "She can fight more."

Beatrice studied her friend. She could see the struggle she was undergoing. She knew that

Louise was not at all prepared for Margaret's death. She wondered if Louise was dealing at all with what was happening.

"Lou, I don't know Margaret's reason for wanting to take this trip, but I seriously doubt it's to gain strength to come home and start taking treatments again. If anything, it seems like something totally opposite to me. It sounds to me like she's making her peace, saying her good-byes, and then she'll come home—"

"I know what it sounds like," Louise interrupted her. "But that's what I pray. That's what you asked me and that's what I pray."

Beatrice backed off. "Okay," she remarked. "I understand. But Lou, at least rethink the promise you're making."

Louise considered what her friend was saying. "What?" she asked.

"I don't really think God would want you to be a television preacher."

Louise got off the stool and headed for the door. "Maybe," she noted. "Or maybe I look really good on camera." She smiled. "Get the van and pick me up after lunch."

"I'm taking care of it," Beatrice said as she opened the door for Louise.

And there was something about the way Beatrice responded that made Louise flinch.

# Pecan Cake

❄❄❄

3 cups sugar
½ cup butter, softened
1 cup shortening
5 eggs
3 cups flour
⅛ teaspoon salt
1 cup milk
2 cups chopped pecans
1 teaspoon vanilla

Cream sugar, butter, and shortening in mixing bowl. Add eggs. Mix well. Combine flour and salt. Add alternately with milk. Stir in pecans and vanilla. Pour into 10-inch Bundt pan. Bake at 300 degrees for 2 hours and 15 minutes.

# Chapter Fourteen

"But why now?" Lana wanted to know. She was visiting Jessie, showing off Hope's pictures taken with Santa Claus.

"James, where's that black suitcase?" Jessie yelled out the door to her husband. She waited for his response before answering her granddaughter-in-law.

"In the closet, on a shelf," he yelled back.

Jessie walked over to the closet and opened the door. She looked on the top shelf and there it was. She reached up to pull it down and felt Lana right beside her. Lana helped her get it from the shelf.

"Thank you, dear," she said as she walked with it over to the bed. "I'm not really sure about why we're going now. I didn't ask her that," she finally answered Lana's question. "Margaret just wanted to go and we're taking her."

Lana nodded. She wanted to ask the obvious question about Margaret's condition and whether this was some end-of-life request but she didn't. She didn't want to pry.

"I really hate that I'm going to miss you on Christmas," Jessie said as she turned to look at Lana. "I love seeing the baby open her presents."

Lana smiled. "It's okay. We'll take lots of

pictures, and besides, you'll be back by next weekend, won't you?"

Jessie nodded. "As far as I know. I don't think we'll get back by Christmas Day but I don't think Margaret intends to stay more than just a couple of days. There's supposed to be a storm coming though; that's why we're leaving today instead of tomorrow."

"Did you find it?" James was walking into the room. "Oh." He was surprised to find Lana sitting on the bed. "I didn't know you were here. Where's Hope?" he asked, looking around the room.

"She's at a party," Lana replied. "In fact, I should go to get her. I just wanted to stop by before you leave and give you the pictures." She got up from her seat.

"Here, let me see that," James took the photographs. "Ah, isn't she just the cutest girl you've ever seen?" He smiled and winked at his grandson's wife.

"I do think that they turned out pretty good." She glanced over the pictures again.

"Well, I guess I should be leaving. We'll miss you, Miss Jessie." Lana reached over and hugged the older woman. "You be safe and we'll see you when you get back."

"Thanks, Lana," Jessie said. "You have a nice Christmas and we'll get together next week-end."

Lana waited before she left. Jessie could see that she had something else to say.

"I'm sorry about Miss Margaret," she said, the tears welling in her eyes.

James walked out of the room. He thought the two women should have the moment alone.

"I know how much I feel about her; I can only imagine what this is like for you."

Jessie hugged Lana again. She felt the tears sting her eyes as well. And she ended the embrace and got a box of tissues from the dresser. She held them out to Lana, who took one, and then pulled one out for herself.

"It's terrible," Jessie confessed. "I go from feeling angry and frustrated to really, really sad." She sat down on the bed, and Lana sat beside her. "I think that's why Louise and Beatrice and I are willing to go on this trip. It's really silly but I just think otherwise we would be too sad to try and face Christmas without some sort of adventure."

Lana nodded. "I think that makes a lot of sense." She wiped her nose. "And Reverend Stewart is going to meet you in Texas?" she asked.

"Yes, that part is really good," Jessie replied. "We all look forward to seeing her."

The young woman smiled. She missed her former minister as well. "Tell her hello for me. And here . . ." She reached in her jacket pocket and pulled out another photograph of Hope. "Give her this. I think she'd like it."

Jessie nodded. "I'm sure she will." She took the photograph and placed it in the pocket of the suitcase that was beside her.

"I just want you to know that I hope I can be as good of a friend as you are to Margaret. I hope that I'll have friends like you do." Lana slid her hands across her legs. "Sometimes I think the girls my age don't care about having friendships. And even me, I get so busy with Hope and Wallace and school, I don't have a lot of time for my girlfriends either. But when I see you and Miss Louise and Miss Bea, the way you care for Miss Margaret, the way you care for each other, it makes me really hope that one day I'll have friends like that too."

Jessie smiled at the young woman and nodded. She put her arm around Lana. "Having a loving and supportive family is a really wonderful thing. I wouldn't trade anything for what I feel for my children and grandchildren." She smiled wider. "And great-grandchildren."

Lana leaned into Jessie.

"But as important as family members are, they can't replace your friends. The really amazing thing about life is that when it comes to surrounding yourself with good people, you can have a vast assortment. You can love your family and you can have friends you can count on. Sometimes these friendships happen when you're young and you just manage to stay together, or sometimes they come along when you get to a certain age. But you know it when you have it. You know which friends are worth keeping, which ones you want to be with you for the rest of your life."

Lana lifted up her head. "When did you know about Margaret?" she asked.

Jessie glanced over at her grandson's wife. She looked so young to the older woman, so innocent. even though she was married and had a child, Jessie thought they were lifetimes apart.

"Margaret and I met when we were about your age, I think. I came home from college and I started going to church where she was a member. And when I went for the first time, I was the only black person there. And I got a few looks."

Lana nodded. She understood what racism felt like. Even though she was white, because she was in a mixed relationship, she had experienced prejudice from both white and black people in the community.

"But Margaret Peele made sure that I was welcomed and warmly received by that church. She was the first person to greet me and she sat with me every Sunday from then on. I didn't know it at the time, but I learned later that she gave quite a lecture to the older adults when they had talked about my being there and what I was trying to do." Jessie shook her head. "Even when she was barely out of high school, she was more woman than I had ever seen."

Lana dropped her head. She knew how hard this was for Jessie to talk about.

"And she has been a friend to me like nobody else. She made me a better person, and I can't think of anything more important to say about another human being. She made me want to be better."

Jessie felt the tears rolling down her cheeks, and she knew that she couldn't start down that emotional road. So she patted her hands together and jumped up from the bed. "Now, I have to pack because Louise and Beatrice will be here soon to pick me up and then we're heading over to Margaret's to go to Texas."

"I'm sorry if I made you sad," Lana confessed.

Jessie turned to the young woman and cupped her hands around her face. "You have never made me sad, dear one. And all you did today was remind me of how incredibly lucky I am to have old friends and young ones in my life."

Lana smiled. She stood up, and the two women hugged.

"Now, you go wrap your presents and bake your cake and hang your stockings because Christmas is almost here."

"Right," Lana agreed. "In fact, I was going to use one of the recipes from the cookbook from the church and bake the pecan cake. Wallace likes pecans and I thought I would use that Bundt pan I got for our wedding and never used."

"Sounds perfect," Jessie responded. "I'll see you when I get back." And she watched as Lana left the room and said good-bye to James.

She started opening drawers and pulling out the things she needed to pack. She felt James behind her before he spoke.

"You okay about this trip?" he asked. He was feeling a little concerned that he had made the women do something that they might not have wanted to do. They hadn't really talked about it since the night Louise had come over and he had suggested it.

She nodded without turning around. "Of course," she finally said.

"Do you want me to go too and drive?" he asked. He knew she was concerned about the weather and the winter storm that was being predicted for that part of the country.

"I think we'll be okay," she replied. "If not, we'll just stop and wait it out," she added.

James turned his wife around and faced her. "Let me look in your eyes when you're telling me this." He studied her.

"We'll be fine," she said. "You were absolutely right about us going to Texas, and I thank you for that."

"But?" James could tell that there was something that his wife wasn't saying. He had felt that way for a few days but he hadn't asked her about it.

"But nothing," she responded. Then she turned

back to the bed and began folding clothes and putting them in the suitcase.

"Jessie Jenkins, I know you better than anybody. Something else is going on for you." He touched her on the arm, and she turned around to face him again. "What is it?" he asked.

She dropped her eyes. He reached up and lifted her chin. "Is it missing Christmas here?" he asked.

She shook her head.

"Are you scared about the weather?"

"No, I told you we can stop if we run into trouble."

"Is it not knowing what you're going to find when you get there?"

Jessie didn't respond to that. She took in a breath and sat down on the bed. James sat down beside her and waited.

"I just don't know what Margaret thinks this trip is going to give her. I just don't understand what we're doing taking her to Texas five days before Christmas." She stretched out her legs and crossed them at the ankles.

"I mean, does she think she'll get some magical answer to things there? Does she think her mother's spirit is there and waiting for her?" She shook her head. "I just don't understand what she's looking for in Goodlett, Texas."

James considered what his wife was saying. He knew how devastated she had been with all that was going on with Margaret. Her heart had not been in any of the holiday events or activities. She had been so low for the past few weeks that he was a bit glad that she was going on the trip. He thought that at least it would give her a new venue to be in. At least it would take her out of Hope Springs.

"Maybe she doesn't know what she's looking for either," he responded. "But just because you don't know for sure what you're looking for doesn't mean you can't find it. Maybe she'll know it when she sees it."

Just as she had put her arm around Lana, James put his arm around Jessie.

"I just hate the thought of her being disappointed," Jessie explained. "Especially now, especially at Christmas," she added.

"I expect she can't hear anything more disappointing than what she's already heard," he said.

Jessie knew that was probably a true statement.

"And what if it isn't what she's hoping for, or what if she feels sadder being there at her mother's grave? Isn't that a part of this process too?"

"What process?" Jessie asked.

"Dying," James replied quietly.

The two didn't speak for a few minutes.

"I just wish I could make a way for her to feel some delight and joy for Christmas. I wish I could give her the perfect gift."

"No, I think what you would like is for this to go away at Christmas," James noted. "But it isn't."

Jessie pulled away a bit from her husband. Even though he was only speaking from his heart, she didn't really want to hear any of it.

"You are giving Margaret the one gift she has been able to ask for. Do you know how amazing that is?" he asked.

Jessie looked at him. Clearly she didn't understand what he was saying.

"First of all, Margaret was able to know what she wanted. So many people spend their whole lives not being able to articulate that, and then when they do come to the end, they have no idea what they need to say good-bye. But Margaret was able to see what was missing, see what she regretted; and she was able to ask her friends to help her get that." He was looking directly into his wife's eyes. "And then you and Louise and Beatrice, even Charlotte, are willing to do this for her. That's unbelievable," he added. "Don't you see that?"

Jessie shook her head. "No, I don't see any of that."

"That's because your heart is broken and your mind is full of sadness. But I see it and it's so beautiful."

"What?" she asked. "Please, help me understand this because I'm not feeling anything beautiful about this. I'm feeling scared and sad and worried."

"Margaret is clear enough to ask for what she needs. And she's blessed enough to have friends in her life that she can ask. She's able to say to you, 'Help make this come true.' And you are open and loving and good enough to say yes." He wiped the tear from Jessie's cheek. "You can't see what a rare and wonderful gift you are giving to your friend?"

"She'd do the same for me," Jessie replied.

"Of course she would," he said. "That's what is so beautiful about this. That's what is so amazing. That's what Lana was asking you about because she doesn't have that in her life, not yet at least." He reached over and wiped a tear from Jessie's cheek.

"Even I don't have anybody like that in my life." He could see the surprise. "I have you," he added, knowing what she was thinking. "But I don't have friends in my life like Louise and Beatrice. I don't have anybody that I could ask to give me something I needed, nobody but family.

"So, you see, it doesn't matter what comes out of this trip. It doesn't matter if Margaret doesn't find the thing she's looking for or even if she doesn't come to some realization of exactly what it is that she's looking for. She's got the best of life already."

Jessie waited for more.

"She's got you. She's got Louise and Beatrice. She's got Charlotte. And I bet that no matter what she finds when she gets to west Texas, she will understand that her greatest gift was not what she found but what she already had."

Jessie turned away.

"You will not bring disappointment or more sadness to Margaret than she is already facing. That's impossible." He squeezed her on the shoulder. "Only goodness and loveliness can come from this adventure. It is rooted in the very best ground. It is rooted in love."

Jessie looked to her husband again.

"There is no better gift for Christmas than the gift you are giving to your friend." He pulled her into him.

"Now, get that suitcase packed because I think I hear Louise and Beatrice coming up the driveway."

Jessie and James both leaned toward the bedroom door where they could see out to the road. Lana had left the front door open, and they both heard the van as it drove up.

"Is there somebody dead on our street?" James asked.

Jessie looked more closely at the vehicle coming up the driveway.

"Lord, have mercy, we're driving to Texas in the funeral home van."

And both of them shook their heads and laughed.

# Oatmeal Cake

❄❄❄

1 cup oatmeal, uncooked
1¼ cups boiling water
½ cup vegetable shortening
1 cup white sugar
1 cup brown sugar
2 eggs and 2 egg whites
1½ cups sifted flour
1 teaspoon nutmeg
1 teaspoon salt
1 teaspoon baking soda
1 cup raisins (if desired)

Mix oatmeal and boiling water and set aside to cool. Mix all ingredients well and add oatmeal mixture. Stir until fairly smooth. Pour into greased 8-inch square pan. Bake at 325 degrees for 30 minutes.

[*continued*]

## TOPPING

1 stick margarine, melted
1 cup brown sugar
1 cup chopped nuts
1 bag of coconut (14 ounces)
2 beaten egg yolks

Add ingredients to melted margarine. Cook about 2 minutes. Spread on cake while hot, and brown in oven.

# Chapter Fifteen

"Don't even say a word." Louise was opening the passenger side door and stepping out of the van. "I have already said everything that can be said."

"I . . . well . . . I . . ." Jessie could only stand on the front porch shaking her head. She didn't even know what to say. She had certainly not considered taking the trip in a van from the funeral home. It was absolutely a shock to her, and she was at a complete loss for words.

"Jessie, it's all I could get on such short notice." Beatrice was opening the driver's side door and walking toward the couple. She was trying to explain her choice before Louise said everything.

"You had five days, Beatrice. We told you on Wednesday that we would need the van on Sunday, five days." Louise was clearly rattled, clearly upset by what Beatrice had done.

"Yes, but it's Saturday!" Beatrice exclaimed. "It's not Sunday, it's Saturday. I could have gotten a van from Hertz tomorrow but they didn't have one today." And that was true, she had tried to find a van.

Louise didn't respond. There was no need. She had checked. None of the rental agencies had any suitable vehicles, and there was nothing they could do about it. She shook her head and stood by the van.

"Aren't you going to say something?" Even though Louise had told her not to say anything, she was hoping her friend would make some comment.

Jessie still did not speak.

James came down the porch, carrying Jessie's suitcase and an ice chest, and walked over beside her. "Well, it is roomy," he said, trying to sound cheerful. He peeked in the back window. "What is it used for, flowers and stuff?" he asked.

Louise rolled her eyes. "It's a funeral home van, James, a funeral home van."

She could not believe that he was going along with the idea so easily. She looked again at the side of the van where "Family Funeral Home" was clearly displayed and shook her head again. She stomped over to Jessie for support.

Beatrice walked around to where James was standing. She opened the back door. "Yes, they use it to transport materials," she replied. "Or they take the staff to meetings and things. It isn't used for dead bodies." She looked over at her friends as if that information would ease things. "You hear me, Louise, it's not for dead people."

"Humph." Louise sighed, waving her hand at Beatrice while turning aside. "Look at what it says on the side," she said sharply.

"So?" Beatrice asked, sounding very innocent.

She turned to James, who was still checking out the vehicle. "And see, I was able to add that third seat and still have room in the back for all of our stuff." She pointed to a third seat that had blankets and pillows placed on it. "That way, if Margaret needs to lie down, there's a place for her to do that." Beatrice was smiling. "And it's brand-new," she added. "Hardly any mileage on it at all. Dick says it rides real smooth. Plus, it's free."

James smiled and nodded. "You are quite the savvy travel arranger, Bea."

Louise made another humph noise. She turned to Jessie, who was still standing on the front steps, still not saying a word. "What do you think, Jessie, you want to try and go after Christmas?" She asked the question in her most concerned voice. "You want to try and drive one of our cars? I think Margaret's car could hold us all comfortably. I know mine is too small." She was thinking out loud. "Maybe we could just take one of our cars to Statesville. I know they have a van there."

Louise looked up at Jessie, still waiting for some kind of response from her.

And then Jessie laughed. She laughed a lot. She laughed so much and so hard that it took a few minutes before she could speak. Louise, James, and Beatrice just stood and watched her. They thought it was very peculiar behavior, and they then glanced around, looking at one another.

James placed the suitcase and ice chest in the

back and shut the door. He headed toward his wife. "You okay, Jess?" he asked.

She blew out a big breath and laughed again. "It's absolutely perfect," she finally said. "Margaret will love it."

Louise turned around to look at the van again and then turned back to face Jessie. Clearly she didn't see the humor in it or how Margaret was going to love driving to Goodlett, Texas, in a funeral home van. She thought it was an exercise in very poor taste.

"Jessie, are you serious?" she asked.

And Jessie laughed some more.

Beatrice, on the other hand, didn't see the irony or the tastelessness in her choice of vehicles. She thought it was a perfect solution to their problem, the problem of not having an appropriate vehicle to drive Margaret to Texas comfortably.

She had tried all morning to find a van for them to rent and there was nothing available except a twenty-foot moving truck from the U-Haul place or a station wagon from the closest car rental place. Apparently the few vans that the local agencies carried were being rented for family holiday trips and there were none available until they got to Statesville, which was about two hours away.

At first, when Dick came home for lunch with the van, having picked it up after a wash and wax, Beatrice didn't consider the possibility of using it;

she was thinking about how she had failed again at her one assignment, how Louise was going to yell at her again about not being able to follow through with her one task.

It wasn't until her husband left, taking the car and leaving the van in the front yard, that Beatrice knew it was the solution she needed. It was like a miracle, she had thought; but of course she had not told that part to Louise. But she did. She really thought it was a miracle, a sign or a gift from God.

She saw Dick pulling away and she ran out the door and started inspecting the vehicle. She looked in all the windows and kicked the tires. She even tried to open the hood and look at the engine, though she knew that she would have no idea of what she was looking at. When she couldn't get the hood open, she just patted it on top.

She continued to examine the vehicle, nodding as she went, and determined that it was big enough for the four women. She could also see that with the third seat installed there would be room enough to allow for a bed in the back for Margaret. It was all clean inside and still had that new car smell that she always liked. She didn't think anything about the sign on the side, designating it as a funeral home vehicle; she thought it was exactly what the women needed. It even had four-wheel drive in case they ran into snow on the roads.

She didn't worry about borrowing it because

she knew that the funeral home had other vans, and she guessed that they wouldn't really miss the one that was parked at the house. She figured that she could just take the van, drive to Texas, and be back by Christmas. She thought that since the owner of the funeral home was taking his family to California for the holidays, Dick wouldn't really be in any trouble because she guessed that no one would really ever find out. He was in charge, after all. So she finished getting ready, called Dick to say good-bye and that she would be home in a few days, loaded her suitcase, and went to pick up Louise.

When Beatrice called Dick to say she was leaving, she didn't mention that she was taking the van. She knew he would have told her no. He would have given a thousand reasons that it was a bad idea, including the one big one: that it wasn't their van. So she decided she would wait until she was out of town to let him know what they were driving, let him know that she had the van. She would call when she got to Asheville or Knoxville, a spot too far from home to have to turn around and drive back. She thought her plan was perfect and she was intending to tell her friends about what she was doing, not sensing that anything would be wrong with any of it.

However, by the time Louise had finished yelling at Beatrice, saying she wouldn't go in that van, and making calls, only to find out what

Beatrice had already told her, that there were no vans available, Beatrice had made no mention of the fact that Dick didn't even know about the use of the vehicle. She knew after hearing everything she had heard, Louise would go crazy if she found out that they were actually stealing the funeral van. So Beatrice decided not to share that part.

After almost an hour of screaming at Beatrice, saying she wouldn't allow Margaret to ride in that van, wouldn't allow Beatrice to drive them in that van, Louise got in the vehicle and agreed to go over to Jessie's. Maybe, she thought, Jessie would have some other idea of how they could get a van. Maybe, she thought, Jessie could make Beatrice see what a ridiculous idea it was to take Margaret to Texas in a funeral home van.

Now, however, Louise realized that Jessie wasn't going to take her side. Jessie thought it was funny. Jessie was going to allow them to drive Margaret to her hometown place somewhere in west Texas in the funeral home van. Louise couldn't even believe it.

She just shook her head and stomped back to the van, got in the passenger side, and shut the door. She was so flabbergasted, she didn't even know what to say. She couldn't believe that Jessie didn't think this was a horrible idea, that Jessie thought this was funny. So she just decided to go with them. The only thing she could think was that maybe Margaret wouldn't notice the sign on the side. Maybe she could hurry out and slide open the side door and Margaret wouldn't see what they were driving. She slid down in the seat, trying to figure out the best way to get that accomplished.

"I even have a little cake," Beatrice said, trying to sound upbeat. "You ready, Jess?" she asked.

Jessie nodded and gave a good-bye kiss to James. He whispered something in her ear and she smiled. She walked over to the side of the van and slid open the door and got in.

Beatrice got into the driver's seat and pulled the seat belt across her shoulders. She turned on the engine. "It's oatmeal, the cake, I mean. It'll be nice for the mornings."

She waited until Jessie was in the seat with her seat belt on. They all waved to James, who was standing on the porch. Jessie blew him a kiss and he smiled.

Beatrice pulled out onto the street and turned the car in Margaret's direction.

"It smells nice," Jessie noted as she glanced around inside the van.

"I know," Beatrice said proudly. "It's new."

Louise looked out the window.

"And you were right, it's real roomy, isn't it?"

"They can carry one hundred arrangements in the back, if they take that seat out, of course." Beatrice pulled to the stop sign and looked in both directions carefully before pulling out.

"One hundred?" Jessie asked. She looked all around the van again and nodded. "It was sure nice of Dick to let us borrow it," she noted.

Beatrice made a kind of humming noise, and Louise turned quickly in her direction.

"Dick does know, doesn't he?" Louise asked.

"Oh my," Beatrice quickly answered. "Do you think we should have packed a thermos of coffee?" She wanted to change the subject as quickly as possible.

"I have one," Jessie replied. "And I brought an ice chest with some sandwiches in it." She knew that James had put it in the back.

"Great!" Beatrice exclaimed. She was glad to talk about food and not about her husband.

"I think this is real nice, Bea," Jessie said.

Louise sighed and shook her head. She still couldn't believe that they were going to pick up their friend, sick with cancer, and drive her to Texas in a funeral home van. It was all just beyond her good senses.

"Oh, come on Lou, it's fitting," Jessie said, reaching up and slapping her friend on the shoulder.

"How is it fitting?" she asked.

"For us," Jessie replied. "It's simply fitting for us." She laughed again.

"We are the cookbook committee," Beatrice added, even though her comment made no sense to anyone.

"Now, I was thinking that we would take turns

behind the wheel," Beatrice announced. "I will drive first and then we can take two-hour shifts. We're staying in Knoxville tonight, right?" She glanced over to Louise.

"That's the plan," she replied.

Suddenly Beatrice made a sharp turn down a side street, slinging Louise and Jessie across their seats. She made the quick turn because she realized that if she went the way she was planning to go, she would have driven right past the funeral home. She certainly did not want to do that. She tried to play off what had happened. "Wheeee," she said, trying to make it seem like she had intended to make the turn.

"Beatrice! What is wrong with you?" Louise was sliding back into her seated position. She had been thrown toward the console stationed between the two front seats.

"Oh, I just remembered how much holiday traffic we would run into if we took River Road over to Hawthorne." Beatrice nervously looked in the rearview mirror, trying to make sure that no one had spotted the van and was following them. She didn't see anything.

"Well, if you're driving like that to Knoxville, your shift is about over," Louise noted. She could tell that Beatrice had gotten nervous about something. She turned around to look behind them.

"So, we'll get to Asheville about five P.M. Do we want to stop there for dinner?" Beatrice asked, trying to distract Louise. “Or will we just eat the sandwiches and cake and keep going?”

“Why don’t we just wait to see when we get hungry or tired of sitting?” Jessie replied. “There’s really no schedule for this adventure. We’ll let Margaret decide how she’s feeling.”

Beatrice nodded. She made the turn down Margaret’s road and then drove into the driveway. When they stopped, Louise jumped out and quickly slid open the side door of the van so that the sign was not visible. She hoped that Margaret wouldn’t walk around to the other side. There was nothing she could do about that sign.

“I’ll go get her,” Jessie said as she stepped out. Louise stood by the door, guarding it. Jessie just shook her head when she realized what her friend was doing. “It won’t matter, Lou,” she said. “She’ll see it eventually. And I promise you, Margaret will think this is a hoot.”

“Whatever,” Louise responded. “But why don’t we wait until we’re out of Hope Springs before we show her what she’s traveling in?”

“Do you want me to help you with her and her stuff?” Beatrice rolled down the window and asked.

“I think we can manage,” Jessie replied.

Jessie walked to the door just as Margaret opened it. The two women smiled at each other.

“Your chariot awaits,” Jessie announced.

And at that moment, Beatrice honked the horn,

scaring Louise and causing her to jump, letting go of the van door, which began to close, clearly exposing the sign she was trying to keep hidden.

Jessie, of course, was right. Margaret thought it was the funniest thing she had ever seen.

# Section Four

# Orange Slice Cake

❄❄❄

2 sticks margarine
2 cups sugar
4 eggs
3½ cups plain flour
½ cup buttermilk
1 teaspoon baking soda
(dissolved in buttermilk)
2 cups chopped pecans
1 pound orange slice candy cut in small pieces
2 pounds dates cut in small pieces
½ cup coconut

Cream margarine and sugar; add eggs one at a time; add flour alternately with milk. Add nuts, candy, and dates rolled in flour. Add coconut. Cook in tube pan at 250 degrees for 2 hours and 30 minutes.

[*continued*]

## TOPPING

1 cup fresh orange juice
2 cups powdered sugar

Mix orange juice and sugar thoroughly and pour over hot cake just removed from the oven. Let stand in pan overnight or for several hours.

# Chapter Sixteen

"We're in Amarillo." Charlotte couldn't hear Jessie very well. They were both on cell phones and there wasn't a very good connection. It was almost lunchtime. She and Rachel had slept late and then eaten a big breakfast. She waited. "Jessie, are you there?"

"Yes, hold on just a minute, let me see if I can get a better signal."

The two women paused.

"Okay, is that better?" she asked.

"Yes, much better," Charlotte replied. "So, where are you guys?" she asked.

They had spoken to each other over the weekend, once on Saturday before they left Hope Springs. And then Charlotte had called Jessie on Sunday evening to tell her that she and Rachel, one of the women from the shelter, were leaving Gallup on Monday morning and would make it to Amarillo to spend the night.

She knew that the group had left North Carolina Saturday evening and were planning to be in Goodlett by Tuesday. She learned, however, from her phone call on Sunday that they had gotten a bit off schedule once they started their trip from Tennessee. Beatrice apparently persuaded them all to stop in Memphis and get a picture of the four of them at Graceland.

Based upon the conversation she had with Louise on Sunday evening, the women had gotten separated at Elvis's estate and Beatrice had gotten locked in the jungle room. There was some sort of trouble with security and they were asked to leave. She couldn't make out the rest of the story, the women were laughing too hard.

However, after the holdup in Memphis, Charlotte wasn't sure that they would make it to Little Rock Sunday night or if they would get all the way to Oklahoma City on Monday night. She hadn't talked to them since just after the Memphis side trip.

Every time Charlotte tried to call Jessie, she was sent directly to her voice mail. She knew that either there had been no good signal for her to return the calls or Jessie had still not quite figured out how to work her cell phone. Regardless, Charlotte was quite relieved to be able to talk to her friend on Tuesday.

"We're almost to Oklahoma City," Jessie replied. "We spent last night in Fort Smith but we got up pretty early to start today. We didn't make it to the hotel Louise had planned for us but we're almost caught up by now. We're about to get on Highway 62. Then we drop down on Highway 83 to hit 287. We should be in Goodlett before it gets dark."

"Louise and Beatrice still fighting?" Charlotte

asked. She was grinning when she asked it.

"Bickering, like old hens," Jessie replied. "But what else is new?" she asked.

"Lou started it," Beatrice said, breaking into Jessie's conversation. "I could have gotten us to Little Rock by nightfall if she hadn't wanted to stay and sing with the Elvis choir."

"I started it?" Louise said. She was driving, and Beatrice was beside her on the passenger side. "You were the one who was locked up in the hall closet in the King's house and stopped all the tours. I was where we were supposed to be, just hanging out in the souvenir shop waiting for you."

"I was ready to leave while you were trying to sneak in the back row of the choir." Beatrice folded her arms across her chest.

"You hear all that?" Jessie asked.

"Has it been that way since North Carolina?" Charlotte asked. She knew how Beatrice and Louise could argue.

Back in Hope Springs she had left them in the church after a meeting one evening fussing about something with each other and found them there the next morning, asleep in the day care center. Charlotte knew that these women could keep an argument running for days.

"How's Margaret doing?" she asked, deciding to change the subject from Beatrice and Louise. She had been concerned that the trip was too much for Margaret. She didn't know the condition of her friend, but knew that Margaret had not been well since she left the hospital.

"She's a trouper," Jessie said. She turned back to look on the seat behind her where Margaret was sleeping.

It was easy to see how frail she appeared, how much weight she had lost in the previous months, but Jessie could also see how peacefully she was resting. She didn't know how her friend could sleep through all the noise in the van.

"We've actually had a lot of fun," Jessie noted with a smile.

And it was true. They had already seen a lot of sights in the three days they had been on the road. They had stopped in Nashville at the Grand Ole Opry and heard a Christmas concert, shopped at some outlet stores in Arkansas, and stopped at the monument in Oklahoma City that was just off the interstate. They had packed a lot into the trip. Memphis and Graceland was just one of many adventures they had shared.

"Tell her about the orange cake," Beatrice said.

"Bea wants me to tell you about this cake we ate in Arkansas. We stopped at some truck stop off the highway and Bea ordered this cake for dessert. It was made with those candy orange slices. You remember those?" Jessie asked.

"Real sugary ones?" Charlotte responded.

"That's them. Anyway, it was certainly a different kind of cake. I didn't care for it myself but Beatrice wouldn't let us leave this diner until she could call the woman who baked this cake and get the recipe. She's pretty excited about it so you may be getting a cake in the mail in the new year."

"She just can't get enough recipes, can she?"

The two of them laughed.

"Well, I'm glad you've been safe and I certainly figured you all would make this trip into something memorable," Charlotte responded. "I hope you have your camera with you."

"We do. And we have some fine photographs of Louise singing with a choir of Elvis look-alikes and Beatrice being escorted off the premises at Graceland by security guards." Jessie laughed.

"I think that one big man with the Santa hat sort of liked me," Beatrice said. She turned around in her seat to face Jessie.

"I think so too, Bea," Jessie said, responding to Beatrice. "We think we may use them for next year's Christmas cards," she said to Charlotte. "So, anyway, we should be in Goodlett by suppertime. You got any idea where we could meet?"

"There's an RV park in Goodlett. It's off the highway going into town. It's got 'cotton gin' in the name of it. We could meet there," Charlotte suggested. "Rachel thought it had a little store, so we could just meet in the parking lot."

"Cotton Gin RV Park," Jessie repeated. She knew about Rachel because Charlotte had mentioned her passenger when they had talked on Saturday.

"Sounds perfect and it shouldn't be hard to locate. We'll plan to see you there in a few hours."

And with that, the signal was gone.

Charlotte placed her cell phone in the console beside her seat.

"You lose her again?" Rachel asked.

"Yeah, or Jessie hit the end button with her chin." She smiled. "I don't think she's quite gotten her cell phone technology figured out yet."

Rachel nodded. "I never used one before."

"Really?" Charlotte asked. "You want to use mine?" she offered, wondering if Rachel had even phoned her sister to let her know she was in Texas.

"Nah," she replied. "I don't even know anybody to call." She slumped down in the passenger seat.

Charlotte and Rachel hadn't talked much since they started the trip the day before. They left after the Christmas party at the shelter. Charlotte thought it had been a nice event for all the women.

She had arranged for a five-course dinner at a semi-upscale restaurant. A local church had paid for it, and all the women had gotten dressed up. None of them had ever eaten at such a nice place, and Charlotte had loved how much the women seemed to enjoy themselves. After dinner, they went back to the shelter, had desserts, and opened presents, which Charlotte had arranged with another charity organization.

The women had all received gift cards, new

coats, some pieces of jewelry, and perfume. And the children, Loretta's three, had all gotten toys and clothes and picture books. Charlotte had worked very diligently to make sure the women were well cared for during the holidays, and it had been a successful endeavor.

She had worked as the executive director of the shelter long enough to know that holidays were difficult for her clients. Most of them didn't have family they could visit and were sad about having to live in a women's shelter. Some of them even commented that they missed their abusers. She knew of some women who even went back into their violent situations just because the holidays were so lonesome for them.

Every year since she had taken the job in Gallup, she tried to make Christmas special and meaningful for the women. She knew that it couldn't take away the difficult circumstances the women were facing, but at least she could give them a little joy, a tiny bit of delight.

Rachel seemed to be the most surprised by the dinner and the presents given at the party. Charlotte noticed that the young woman struggled through the dinner, appearing as if she was uncomfortable eating in such a fancy place. The other women seemed to notice it too, and they all tried to make her feel more at home. Then when they all went back to the shelter and received their gifts, Rachel had not opened any of hers with the rest of the group. She had taken them all back to her room.

Charlotte didn't know when she opened them, but she knew that Rachel was wearing the new coat, and she thought she could smell perfume on the young woman. She hadn't said anything to Rachel when she left the party without opening her gifts. No one had. All the women knew that sometimes for a victim of violence, goodness can feel overwhelming. They had simply left her alone.

"Why did you come out here from North Carolina?" Rachel asked.

The radio was tuned to a station that was playing Christmas music. Charlotte liked the songs but she turned the radio down a bit since her passenger seemed interested in having a conversation.

"I don't know really," Charlotte replied. "I read a book about the Southwest. It had a lot of pictures in it of the landscapes and the different pueblos and the sky, and it explained a lot about the history of the place. I had dreams about living in the desert. I just knew I wanted to live out here even before I ever saw it."

"That's weird," Rachel responded.

"I guess so."

"You still feel that way about it?"

Charlotte nodded. "More so. It's exactly what I thought it would be, only it's more. It's like home, only it's brand-new." She smiled thinking about her move to the Southwest, how odd it felt to leave

North Carolina, how right it felt to be where she was.

"Do you like New Mexico?" Charlotte asked.

Rachel shook her head. "Not really."

"Where would you like to live then?" she asked.

"I guess Texas," the young woman replied. "That's the only place I know real good."

"And what do you like about Texas?" Charlotte asked.

Rachel considered the question. Charlotte could tell that the teenager had never thought about her home state.

She shrugged. "I guess it's home. I know where everything is here, what people think about, what's important to them. I could never seem to feel that way in New Mexico."

"Did you like growing up here?" Charlotte asked. She was hoping that Rachel might open up a bit with her since she had not shared anything about her life since moving into the shelter.

Rachel nodded. She glanced out the window.

They had taken the turn off the interstate and were heading south from Amarillo down to Childress. There were miles and miles of empty fields. They passed a few barns, a few houses situated far off the road. There were some oil pumps and a few head of cattle. They passed hardly any other cars on the road. It was quite a desolate place.

"It was hard, I mean. We were pretty poor.

Grandma just got a welfare check and Uncle Nestor helped us as much as he could but we just never had much. Sometimes I felt bad about that. But mostly I didn't care."

Charlotte glanced over at her passenger. She seemed so old and yet she was still so young. Charlotte wondered if there was violence in her childhood too. She knew there were often patterns repeated in the lives of victims of domestic violence. She wondered if Rachel had ever talked about it.

"So, what about Childress do you miss?" Charlotte asked.

Rachel smiled. She had thought about that. She had thought about that a lot. "There's a way that the wind sounds in west Texas. I've never heard it anywhere else. It's like a woman's voice." She fidgeted with her seat belt. "My sister was always afraid of it; she thought it was a ghost or something. But I always liked it. Made me think of my mamma and her singing to me."

Charlotte wanted to ask more about the young woman's mother but she decided just to let her talk. She knew that Rachel was considering the prospect of seeing a counselor, and Charlotte was glad that Rachel was thinking about getting professional help. She decided to let her passenger talk as much or as little as she wanted. She would not push the conversation to such a deep level.

"Tell me what you used to do for Christmas."

Charlotte thought that was an innocent direction in which to steer their talk.

"They were kind of fun," she replied.

"Yeah?" Charlotte asked, waiting for more.

"Yeah. My sister and me would start early on Christmas Eve and we would go to all of the churches in town. Grandma never really liked what we did but she didn't make us stop." Rachel smiled as she remembered.

"They always give out bags of candy and fruit at the local Methodist church. And the Baptist church gave out bags of groceries. The AME Zion church made homemade pies and cookies, and then we would go to the fancy church downtown for a wrapped present. It would usually be some doll or maybe a book. But it was nice."

Charlotte nodded. She had never thought about families going from church to church to gather up holiday supplies. Once she heard the idea, however, it made sense. In a way, that was sort of what she did as an executive director of a women's shelter. She would go through the yellow pages, getting phone numbers of local churches, and then call and ask for specific donations.

"It sounds like you were pretty resourceful as a child," Charlotte noted.

"Oh yeah, my sister and me learned how to work the holidays."

The two women were silent for a while as they drove along the highway.

"What about you?" Rachel asked. "What did you do for Christmas? Did you have a big family gathering and lots of presents?"

Charlotte began to think about her childhood holidays. She thought about her sister and how long it had been since she considered what it had been like growing up in her mother's house. Even though she had been the one to start the conversation, she hadn't thought that it would involve her own secrets.

"Well, if my mother was on the wagon, we could have a pretty good time," she explained. "She'd cook and we'd have a nice dinner like normal families. We'd go to church on Christmas Eve and usually we'd get a present or two from Santa Claus."

Rachel nodded. She was watching Charlotte closely. "And if she fell off of the wagon?" she asked.

"Then you just never knew what Christmas was going to be like." Charlotte held the steering wheel with her right hand and then dropped her elbow against the car door and leaned into her left hand. These were the memories she hadn't considered in a long time. These were the memories she tried to forget.

"I guess everybody's recovering from one thing or another, huh?" Rachel asked.

And Charlotte glanced over at her passenger, who was looking at her as if she had made a new friend.

# Chocolate Cookie Cake Sheet

❄❄❄

2 cups flour
2 cups sugar
½ teaspoon salt
1 teaspoon baking soda
1 cup water
2 tablespoons cocoa
½ cup oil
1 stick margarine
2 eggs, beaten
½ cup buttermilk
1 teaspoon vanilla

In a large bowl, sift together flour, sugar, salt, and baking soda. In saucepan, combine and boil water, cocoa, oil, and margarine. Pour into dry ingredients. Add eggs, buttermilk, and vanilla. Pour into ungreased 15 x 10 x 1–inch pan and bake at 350 degrees for 20 to 25 minutes.

[*continued*]

## ICING

1 stick margarine
2 tablespoons cocoa
⅓ cup milk
1 box powdered sugar
1 teaspoon vanilla
1 cup pecans (optional)

Combine margarine, cocoa, and milk in saucepan. Heat until margarine melts, then add powdered sugar, vanilla, and nuts. Pour over hot cake.

# Chapter Seventeen

"Is this the place?" Charlotte was getting out of her car. They had parked in front of the small RV park that was the designated spot to meet up with the women from Hope Springs. The sun was dropping and it had turned colder.

"This is it," Rachel replied. She seemed a bit excited, and even though she still shifted carefully and slowly because of her recent injuries, Charlotte hadn't seen her move as quickly as she did as she emerged from the passenger side.

Charlotte noticed how much more energetic she seemed, and she stood watching the young woman.

"What?" Rachel asked, uncomfortable with the sudden attention.

"Why don't you go in and see if your friend is still around?" Charlotte asked.

Rachel started biting her lip and turned away. She glanced toward the RV office and small general store that was only a few hundred yards away.

"Well, it can't hurt just to go in and ask about the guy," Charlotte said. She could tell that Rachel was very curious about her old boyfriend.

"I don't know," she said, still biting her lip. She pushed her hair behind her ears and shifted her weight from side to side. She flinched when she leaned on the right side. She was still badly bruised from the broken bones she had suffered.

"Well, it can't hurt to go in and ask," Charlotte repeated. "That's what you're doing here, right?"

The young woman didn't answer.

"Oh for heaven's sake," Charlotte said. "Do you want me to go in there and ask?"

"No," Rachel answered quickly. "I can do it myself."

Charlotte waited. "Well," she said.

"I'm going," Rachel responded. And she headed toward the office.

Charlotte watched the young woman as she slowly moved away from the car and to the office door. She turned back to look at Charlotte, who waved her inside. Rachel wasn't looking when someone inside pulled open the door. Charlotte watched as Rachel almost fell. She started to move to the office to help but then she saw the young woman quickly recover and stand back up. Charlotte stayed at the car.

The sky was growing darker and the clouds were thickening. The temperature had kept dropping all afternoon ever since they left Amarillo. She knew that the storm that had caused Jessie and the others to leave a day early was now predicted to come across Texas sometime that night. She worried that it would include ice and that it could keep them from being able to visit the locations that Margaret was eager to visit or that it might prevent them from returning to their homes.

She decided, however, not to worry about it. She knew there was nothing she could do about the weather anyway. She had passed several hotels in Childress, which was just fifteen miles up the road, so she figured they'd be fine even if they had to spend their Christmas in a highway motel. She knew that she would be with women she loved, and as long as Louise and Beatrice were along, she would find something to laugh about.

As she stood looking at the sky, she glanced up the highway and noticed a van coming very fast in her direction. It sped right past her, and when Charlotte saw the sign on the side, "Family Funeral Home, Hope Springs, North Carolina," she blinked and rubbed her eyes. By the time she had taken in the information she had just encountered, the van had sped up to the next driveway, squealed the wheels, turned around, and was heading back in her direction.

When the van pulled into the RV park parking lot, Charlotte was shaking her head in disbelief. She knew that the women were traveling in a van but she had no idea that they were driving a vehicle from the funeral home. Since she knew about Dick's employment, she realized Beatrice was behind the selection. She looked more closely through the windshield as they pulled in beside her and saw that it was Bea driving.

"Nice wheels," was all she could think of to say once the vehicle had parked and the women began piling out of the van.

"You know, actually it rides real smooth when me and Jessie are driving," Louise responded. She was used to the idea of the funeral van by the time they had gotten to Texas but she still thought Beatrice was a bad driver. "How are you, Preacher?" she asked with a big smile spreading across her face.

Charlotte smiled and gave Louise a big hug. "I'm great," she replied.

Beatrice and Jessie then got out of the van and delivered their greetings as well. It was a sweet reunion for them all.

"You look skinny," Beatrice said, sizing up the young woman. Beatrice was wearing a Santa hat. She had bought it back in Arkansas and had been wearing it for most of the trip. "You need something to eat," she added.

Charlotte laughed. "I'm sure you'll figure out a way to fix me up before you leave," she said.

"Turn around and let me get a good look at you." Jessie had her hands up in the air. Charlotte ran over and gave her friend a huge embrace. She whispered in her ear, "I'm so glad you're here."

"Help me! Jessie, somebody, get me out!"

All the women turned to look at the rear of the van. The side door was slid open but no one could see Margaret. Jessie walked to the rear of the van and opened the back doors. Margaret was lying on the backseat. There was a bungee cord wrapped around the end of the seat.

"Why is she strapped in?" Charlotte asked.

"She kept sliding off," Beatrice replied. "So we put the cord over her legs." She walked over to where Jessie was standing, holding open the door. "It's nice, isn't it?" She was quite proud of the vehicle and all its roominess. "You can take out the seats too. Plus look at all of this space for our bags." She opened the door wider to show Charlotte.

"Yes, Bea, it's real nice, but I think Margaret wants to get up."

"Oh, right." Beatrice turned around and unhooked the bungee cord. "Do you want me to move all of the pillows?" she asked.

There were lots of pillows and blankets on the floor in front of the rear seat. Apparently, Charlotte thought, these were put in place in case Margaret did fall forward.

Margaret was huffing. "No, I can get out with them still there." And she rolled over, pushing herself out of the seat. She crawled out the side door. "Whew, I can see why only dead people ride back there," she said.

Beatrice was about to contradict her but then Margaret glanced over and saw Charlotte. "My Lord," was all she said.

Charlotte smiled and ran over to hug her friend.

The two stood in an embrace for a long time. Charlotte was trying not to cry, but she was so full of emotion that she couldn't help herself. She could feel how thin Margaret had gotten. She could sense her weakness.

"Okay, there, that's enough," Margaret said as she pulled herself away from the young woman. "I'm glad to see you too," she added.

Charlotte quickly wiped her eyes and stood away from Margaret.

"So, what is this place?" Louise asked, glancing around.

There were only a couple of motor homes parked in the RV spaces. The general store was the main part of an old mill and included a small sunroom on one side of the building that seemed to house a Jacuzzi as well as the restrooms. The women could see a pool just behind the office.

"It was the only landmark Rachel could remember in the town," Charlotte replied. She wondered if the young woman had found her old boyfriend since she was taking such a long time inside.

"That the young girl you brought with you?" Beatrice asked.

Charlotte nodded. "She's from Childress, so I asked her if she wanted to ride along." She looked over at Margaret again. She was so glad to see her friend. "It was nice to have some company for the trip."

Margaret smiled and nodded.

"What's the weather report?" Jessie wanted to know.

"The storm is supposed to be on its way. It will probably bring some ice and snow with it, but hopefully it isn't supposed to last too long and it's supposed to move north instead of east or west; so that's good for our travels back home."

Jessie nodded.

"You see any places to stay up the road?" Louise asked. She had made all the hotel reservations up until this part of the trip. She was counting on Charlotte to find them rooms now that they were in Texas.

"There are a few hotels in Childress. We shouldn't have any problem finding a place."

It was then that Rachel came out of the office. She was moving slowly and the women watched as she approached.

"She's a little bitty thing, isn't she?" Beatrice asked. "I know that child needs some good cooking."

"Rachel, these are my friends from North Carolina," Charlotte began the introductions. "This is Jessie, Beatrice, Louise, and this is Margaret," she said as she pointed to each woman.

Rachel smiled and said hello to each of them.

"And this is Rachel," Charlotte said.

"It's very nice to meet you." Margaret spoke first. "And I hear that you're from around here too?" she asked.

"Yes ma'am," she replied. "Up the road about ten miles. You come from here?" she asked Margaret.

"No, my mother did," she responded.

Rachel nodded. She remembered how Charlotte had explained the reason for the women traveling to Texas from North Carolina.

"What was her name?" Rachel asked.

"Elizabeth," Margaret replied. "Elizabeth Hearnes."

Rachel shook her head. "I didn't hear of her," she said.

Margaret smiled. "What about your people, what are their names?"

"Lewiston," she replied. "I come from the Lewiston family."

Margaret nodded.

"You find out where your boyfriend is?" Charlotte asked.

"He ain't a boyfriend," Rachel replied. She grinned. "It's his daddy still running the place though." She looked over to the office. "Ricky is in Iraq," she added. "Joined the army a couple of years back."

Charlotte nodded. She wondered if the young woman was upset that her friend wasn't in Goodlett. She studied Rachel but didn't seem to notice any disappointment.

"They got a few of them little camping cabins behind the office. Mr. Workman said that we could stay in them if we didn't want to drive to

Childress." She looked around at the women. "I told him about ya'll coming from North Carolina to see your people," she explained.

"That was very nice of you," Jessie said. She tried to peer around the office but the cabins couldn't be seen from where they stood in the parking lot.

"That was lovely, Rachel," Beatrice noted.

"He said that the storm was rolling in this evening and that he didn't think we should be driving back and forth even if it is only a few miles." Rachel was studying the women. She wasn't sure if they wanted to skip a hotel room for a camping cabin.

"Well, let's go take a look at the accommodations," Margaret suggested. "I don't mind staying here in a cabin. In fact, I think that might be nice."

Louise glanced around. She used to stay in quite a few campgrounds when she had been younger. She thought this one looked nice enough, even though she wasn't ready to commit until she had a better look at the facilities.

The women headed over to the office. The small building was decorated with red and green streamers. A Christmas tree was placed in the corner, next to a fireplace. A fire was burning, and the room smelled of wood. There were a couple of stockings hanging on the mantel and there was Christmas music playing.

"Merry Christmas," the man behind the counter said as the women walked in.

"Merry Christmas to you." Jessie spoke for the group.

The man was in his fifties, broad-chested, and was wearing a sweatshirt that read, "Santa's Back," and had a picture of the back of Santa Claus underneath the words. He winked at Rachel. "Welcome to Goodlett," he added.

"Thank you," Charlotte responded. "We hear you have some cabins that we could rent for a night."

"We got 'em," the man answered. "Brand-new ones, just built. They got heat and two single beds in each of them. There's a small sink and a chest of drawers for your things."

He glanced around at all the women. "I guess you'd need to rent all three of them, which is fine because they're available." He reached behind the counter and pulled out keys. "I'll give you the code to the restrooms but you don't need to worry. The only two units here for the week have their own toilets. So you'd have the facilities to yourselves."

Charlotte smiled.

"Hot tub works. Just cleaned it out. Bathing suits are optional." He grinned.

"I've been staying with these women for a couple of nights. You don't want to go there, trust me," Louise responded.

The man winked again. "And I'll have

doughnuts and coffee in the morning," he added. "Will you be staying through Christmas?" he asked.

The women shrugged.

"Not sure," Jessie answered.

"There any good place to eat in Goodlett?" Beatrice asked. It was getting time for supper and her stomach was starting to growl.

"You can get dinner over at Mac's Diner just up the road before you get to the Methodist church. He makes a good fish dinner or you can try his chicken fried steak. And since it's Christmas this week, he's got chocolate cake." The man waited. "Ya'll like cake?" he asked.

The women all moaned at the same time. Clearly they had all had enough cake to last them an entire season.

"Well, dinner, cake, and a cabin sound perfect." Jessie was the one to speak for the group again.

"Best place to stay in Goodlett," the man responded. He grinned another wide grin at the women. "Which one of you got people here?" he asked.

The women all looked over at Margaret.

"That would be me," she replied, stepping forward.

The man studied her. He could see that she wasn't well. "You a Richardson?" he asked.

Margaret shook her head.

“ ’Cause you look a little like the Richardsons.”

Margaret shook her head again.

Rachel answered for her. “She’s a Hearnes,” she noted. “Her mamma was Elizabeth Hearnes.”

“She kin to Donald?” the man asked.

“That was my grandfather’s name,” Margaret replied, sounding surprised.

The man nodded. “I’m Maurice Workman.” He leaned across the counter and held out his hand. “I think we might be family,” he added.

Margaret smiled and took his hand. “Well, how about that?” she asked.

“My daddy’s mother’s brother married Donald’s sister’s girl.” He paused. “Her name was Eugenia.”

Margaret looked a bit confused. She had researched some of her family history but she didn’t remember the names of her grandparents’ siblings. She had learned her mother’s immediate family but that was all.

She considered what Maurice was saying. “So, I guess that makes us . . .” She thought about it.

“Related,” Maurice interrupted her. He grinned. “I’ll just call you cousin,” he noted. “Cousin . . .” He waited for her to introduce herself.

“Margaret,” she said.

“Cousin Margaret,” he repeated.

“Do you know if any of my people are still around?” she asked.

He thought about her question. “I can ask

Florrie," he replied. "Florrie is my wife and she keeps the records for the Methodist church. She knows about every family in Goodlett."

Margaret smiled. "Is that the little church with the cemetery behind it?" she asked. She wondered if that was the village church she remembered from her one visit to Texas. She wondered if the church was still there.

Maurice nodded. "That's the only church in town," he replied. "And the only cemetery. I suspect your grandparents are buried there. Did your mother have siblings?" he asked.

"She had two sisters," Margaret responded. She did remember that part of her family history.

"I'll ask Florrie if she knows your aunts. Maybe some of their kin is still around. Goodlett isn't that big, you know," he added with a wink.

"I know," Margaret responded.

She took in a breath, and Maurice noticed how tired she looked. "Let me show you a cabin and you and your friends can decide if you want to stay here or drive over to Childress." He took the set of keys he had pulled out and walked around to where the women were standing. " 'Course, now that we know we're related, I think you'll need to stay right here."

Margaret smiled.

"Just follow me and I'll give you a peek at the finest accommodations in Goodlett, Texas." He headed to the door and opened it.

The women walked past him and out the door toward the cabins behind the office.

"Mr. Workman, isn't this the only place to stay in Goodlett?" Rachel asked.

The man smiled. "Well, we don't need to be specific about that kind of thing," he responded. "Besides, there's no better place in the world to be at Christmas," he added, as the door shut behind him.

# Aunt Maymie's Chocolate Syrup Cake

❄❄❄

½ cup butter or margarine
1 cup sugar
4 eggs
1¼ cups flour
1½ teaspoons baking powder
¾ can chocolate syrup (1 pound can)
1 teaspoon vanilla

Cream butter and sugar together until light and fluffy. Add eggs one at a time, beating well after each addition. Sift flour and baking powder together. Add flour mixture alternately with chocolate syrup and vanilla to creamed mixture. Beat well. Pour batter into 2 greased and floured 9-inch cake pans. Bake at 350 degrees about 30 minutes or until done.

[*continued*]

# ICING

15 large marshmallows
5 ounces evaporated milk
2 cups sugar
1 stick margarine
1 6-ounce package of chocolate chips
1 teaspoon vanilla

Combine marshmallows, evaporated milk, sugar, and margarine and bring to a boil, cooking 3 minutes. Remove from heat and add chocolate chips and vanilla. Beat until creamy.

# Chapter Eighteen

The women decided to stay at the RV park and rent the three cabins. Beatrice and Louise were in the one closest to the office. Jessie and Margaret took the middle one. Charlotte and Rachel had the one the farthest away from the facilities. They all agreed that the youngest women would have the least amount of trouble walking to and from the bathroom. Although once that had been agreed upon, they all worried about the young woman who seemed to walk so carefully.

Once they got settled, putting the linens on the beds and unpacking, they rested for a bit and then decided to eat dinner at the place Maurice had mentioned. They all loaded into the funeral van. Charlotte had already heard the story of Beatrice's choice of vehicle. Once they started their short trip to the diner, Charlotte agreed with her friends that it was a comfortable ride.

The temperature had dropped at least ten degrees since they arrived in Goodlett and it was now below the freezing mark. Clouds filled the evening sky, and the women huddled together in the van as they drove to the diner.

There were only a few people inside the small restaurant. There were two deputies enjoying their dinner and a woman with two small children just coming out as the women were going in. They waited for the family and then hurried inside and took a table in the center of the room.

"It is really cold out there," Charlotte noted as she unwrapped the scarf from around her neck.

"Cold enough to make snow stick," Louise added. She was starting to get concerned about the storm and whether they would be able to leave Texas now that they had made it there.

"Are you getting worried?" Beatrice asked as she took her seat and began peeling off her gloves. She still had on her Santa hat and was looking quite festive.

"I just don't know if we want to spend a week in a cabin in Goodlett, Texas," she replied.

"Oh, we'll be fine," Jessie said. She had taken the menus and passed them out to all the women. "Just order something hearty and you'll feel better."

A waitress walked over to take the orders. She was young, not much older than Rachel. She chewed gum and wore a red bow in her hair. She also had on earrings that lit up, a pair of reindeer with bright, shining noses.

"Ya'll know what you want or you need a minute?" she asked.

"You got cake?" Beatrice asked. She winked at Louise.

"Yes ma'am," the girl answered, not knowing that her customer was just trying to be humorous.

"Oh please," Louise said, under her breath.

The waitress didn't hear her. "We got a chocolate cookie cake, and we got the house special." She waited.

"Which is?" Beatrice was interested.

"A chocolate syrup cake," the waitress replied. "It's real rich," she added. "But it's good if you like that kind of thing."

"Oh, I'd say we all like that kind of thing," Jessie responded.

Louise just rolled her eyes and held the menu over her face. Clearly she had eaten enough cake.

All the women ordered and handed their menus to Jessie, who placed them between the salt and pepper shakers situated on the corner of the table. Beatrice glanced around and noticed that the deputy facing her seemed to be eyeing the group. She smiled at the young man but he didn't respond. She watched as he participated in a call on his walkie-talkie, which was attached to a shoulder harness. It wasn't long before the two men got up and left their table.

Louise watched them leave and noticed Beatrice as she followed them with her eyes. "What's the matter?" she asked.

Beatrice turned to her friend. "Nothing," she replied. "I was just thinking about Dick and wondering if he got supper tonight," she added.

"Have you talked to him since we left?" Jessie

asked. She had managed to get through to James all three evenings they had been away.

Beatrice shook her head. Every time she tried to call, the line was busy or there was no answer. She thought about calling the funeral home but she didn't really want to talk to Betty. It wasn't a huge deal that she hadn't contacted Dick. She had left a couple of messages on the home phone saying that they were fine, telling him where they were staying.

In all the time away from home, she hadn't really worried about the fact that she hadn't told him about borrowing the van. She hadn't even really thought about it since leaving North Carolina. She had actually forgotten that he didn't know.

She watched the deputies as they pulled out of the parking lot. The car stopped behind the women's parking place, but none of the other women noticed it.

"So, Rachel." Beatrice turned to the young woman seated across the table from her. "You're from around here?" she asked.

Rachel's face reddened as all the women looked at her. She didn't like having that much attention on her. "Yes ma'am, from Childress," she replied, and dropped her eyes away from the group.

"Beatrice, you look like you've lost some weight." Charlotte was trying to divert the attention away from her young friend. She knew it was uncomfortable for her. "Have you been exercising?" she asked. She knew that Beatrice would love to talk about herself. And she was right.

"Depression," she replied, in a very matter-of-fact style. She lifted the top of her Santa hat away from her face. "It's great for dieting."

Charlotte was surprised by the answer. Since Beatrice brought up the subject, she thought it was fine to follow up. "You've been depressed?" she asked.

"She gave up the cookbook project," Louise said.

The waitress brought out the drinks and passed them out to the women around the table. They were her only customers now that the deputies had left.

"Beatrice!" Charlotte said in a very surprised tone of voice. "You gave up a project? Were you hospitalized?" she asked, and then smiled. "Did they give you electric shock therapy?"

"Very funny," Beatrice replied. "No, I was not hospitalized."

"Turns out all she needed was a kick in the butt from her friends," Jessie said.

"And a patch on her butt from her doctor," Louise added.

"It's the hormones, dear," Beatrice said in Rachel's direction.

Again, the young woman's face reddened.

"You'll learn one day too. Getting old isn't for

sissies." Beatrice took a sip from her glass of iced tea.

"And you're better now?" Charlotte asked.

"Much better. I was a little low on my estrogen," Beatrice noted.

"A little low?" Louise asked. "You were on your way to the psychiatric ward if you didn't get some help."

Charlotte laughed and shook her head in Rachel's direction. "They're best friends," she said.

The young woman nodded, looking a bit suspicious.

"So, how are Wallace and Lana and little Hope?" Charlotte asked. She was hoping to catch up on all the community news.

"Great," Jessie replied, pulling from her purse the picture that Lana had given her to share with Charlotte. "Growing like a weed," she added, speaking of the little girl.

"And school for Lana, how's that?" Charlotte asked as she looked at the photograph. She was smiling at how much Hope had grown and how cute she looked sitting on Santa's knee.

"Making real good grades," Jessie responded.

"She'll be an excellent nurse," Margaret added. It was the first thing she had said since they arrived at the diner.

All the women glanced over at her. They were glad to hear her participate in the conversation.

They had all noticed that she seemed happy to be in Goodlett, but that she was also growing more and more fatigued.

"Oh, she is still a cutie," Charlotte commented.

"Can I see?" Rachel asked.

Charlotte showed her the photograph. She smiled.

"This your granddaughter?" she asked Jessie, giving the picture back to Charlotte.

"Great-granddaughter," Jessie replied. "Her mother married my grandson," she added.

Rachel nodded.

"Charlotte married them," Jessie noted.

Rachel turned to look at Charlotte. She had not known that Charlotte was a minister. She knew that she used to work in a church but she never considered that Charlotte could have been an ordained minister, not that she really understood what that meant.

"You married them?" she asked, looking confused.

"I officiated at the marriage," Charlotte explained. "I was the pastor of the church where they attend."

Rachel nodded. She was starting to understand.

"And you all went to her church?" Rachel asked.

The women nodded.

"Why did you quit being a pastor?" Rachel wanted to know.

The women waited to hear how Charlotte was

going to answer. They all thought they knew the reasons, but no one was really completely sure they understood why the young woman had left her work in the church.

Charlotte could feel all the eyes on her. "I guess I figured most of the folks in church didn't need me so much. And I think I like to be needed. So, I decided to go somewhere else where I thought I could do a little more, make more of a difference."

The women considered her response. It made sense to them all even though they missed having her in Hope Springs.

"And you picked New Mexico because you had a dream?" Rachel recalled the conversation they had as they drove into Texas.

"That's right," Charlotte replied.

"And how is it for you?" Jessie asked. She and the young pastor had talked about the transition, and she thought she could tell it had been a good change for Charlotte; but she wanted to hear an update, hear how it was five years after leaving North Carolina.

"Well, aside from missing all of the cookbook projects"—she smiled over in Beatrice's direction—"I'd say it's been perfect."

Margaret nodded at her young friend. She could tell how happy Charlotte was doing the work she did, living in the place she lived. She was very glad that Charlotte enjoyed her work and she was very pleased to have the opportunity to see her, to be with her in Texas.

The food arrived and they all sat with their plates in front of them. They all turned to Charlotte, who reached out her hands. All the women took hands, including Rachel, who seemed a bit out of place with the religious demonstration.

Everyone closed her eyes except Rachel. She watched as Charlotte led the prayer.

It was short, mostly making note of the food and the traveling mercies they had all enjoyed. But Rachel watched Charlotte as she prayed, and she saw the young woman when she opened her eyes and looked at Margaret. As if being called out, Margaret had opened her eyes and looked too. At that part of the prayer, Charlotte thanked God for friends and for the allowance of possibilities to find peace. The two women smiled slightly at each other as Rachel then bowed her head. She knew it was a private moment between the two and she didn't want to intrude.

Once the prayer was over, the women ate their dinner. Everyone finished at about the same time except Margaret and Rachel. Both of them seemed to have more difficulty eating. Margaret was slow just because she had no appetite and was eating only because she knew she needed the nourishment. Rachel was slow because her jaw had only recently healed after being broken. It was still very painful to chew.

"Do you have a toothache?" Beatrice asked Rachel, having noticed her wincing every time she bit down.

Rachel shook her head.

"Is it the steak?" Beatrice asked. She had ordered the fish, and she wondered how the steak tasted. "Is it tough?"

Rachel shook her head again.

Charlotte thought about trying to divert the conversation, worried that she should try to save Rachel from Beatrice's line of questioning, but before she could switch subjects, Rachel seemed ready to answer.

"I got beat up by my boyfriend," she replied. She turned to Charlotte, who just looked at her. "He broke my cheekbone."

She was surprised that the young woman had decided to answer so honestly.

"Why did he do that?" Beatrice asked. She had never met anyone who claimed to be a victim of violence.

Rachel shrugged as she continued to try and finish her supper.

"Bea." Jessie tried to stop her friend from asking too many questions.

"What?" she asked, understanding what Jessie was trying to do. "It's a fair question, don't you think?"

"It's not really fair for Rachel," Louise noted.

"Why?" Beatrice asked.

"Because she probably doesn't know the reason she was struck," Jessie responded.

"Is that true?" Beatrice asked. She was not getting the message from her friends to stop her questions. She didn't think of herself as a busybody. "Do you not know why he hit you?"

Rachel finished eating and wiped her mouth with her napkin. "I forgot the potted meat," she replied.

"What?" Louise asked. She sounded shocked to hear the answer.

"He was mad because I had gone to the store and forgotten to get his potted meat," she explained. "So he got out the baseball bat and he hit me across the face, crushed my jaw, then he hit me across the back and he broke my hip. And I landed in the hospital for about a month."

The women were silent around the table. They didn't know the stories of violence that Charlotte had become accustomed to. They had no idea that a person could suffer so much for something so trivial.

"And yet, you survived," Margaret said. She had finished her meal by then too. "Look at you. You are to be honored. You're strong and you're sitting at a table eating dinner," she added. "You survived."

Rachel peered at the woman who had taken as long to eat as she had and smiled. She had not thought of her survival as a cause for celebration. She had not thought that her coming through such a violent rage was reason for any honor. But somehow, with the way this woman said what she said, the way she looked at her, Rachel suddenly felt better about herself. She felt taller, stronger. She nodded.

"You did the right thing," Beatrice responded.

All the women turned to her. They didn't know what she was talking about. Rachel seemed confused.

"You should never buy potted meat." She was taking out money from her wallet to cover her meal.

She looked up, and all the women were staring at her.

"What?" she asked. "You all don't buy potted meat, do you?" She looked at her friends. "I mean, even the name is disgusting. Who ever heard of meat in a pot?"

Rachel was the first one to let out a giggle, and soon they were all laughing so hard, the cook had come out from behind the counter to get a look at who was making all the racket.

"Beatrice, you are something," Jessie said.

The women all got up from their table. They put on their coats and gloves and scarves and went over to pay the waitress for their meals. It wasn't until they walked outside and were gathered in the parking lot, just about to get in the van, that they heard all the sirens and saw the police cars moving in their direction.

"Must be an accident down the road," Jessie said.

And then, within seconds, three cars had pulled in surrounding them and six policemen had jumped out and were pointing their guns in the direction of the stunned women.

# *Apple Pound Cake*

❄❄❄

2 cups sugar
1½ cups vegetable oil
3 large eggs
3 cups flour
1 teaspoon baking soda
1 teaspoon salt
1½ teaspoons vanilla
3 cups diced apples
¾ cup flaked coconut
1 cup chopped nuts

Mix sugar and oil; add eggs and beat well. Combine flour, baking soda, and salt and add to oil mixture. Stir in vanilla, apples, coconut, and nuts and mix well. Spoon batter into greased 9-inch tube pan. Bake at 325 degrees for 1 hour and 20 minutes or until cake tests done.

# Chapter Nineteen

The funeral van had been reported stolen in North Carolina not long after the women left on the Saturday before Christmas. Dick got home after running a few errands that afternoon and noticed as soon as he pulled in his driveway that the vehicle was gone. He called the police and filed a report right away.

He figured the thief had been watching the house and assumed that no one was at home, that the family was away for the holidays. He talked to the officer who had been dispatched to his house and gave a very detailed report about the model, make, and condition of the business vehicle. He chose not to call the owner of the funeral home, thinking that the stolen van was not cause to ruin a family's holiday. He thought they would possibly recover the van before his boss returned.

It never crossed Dick's mind that his wife had taken the new funeral van to Texas. He knew there were more thefts during the holidays than any other time of the year, and he just thought he had been a victim. Since he had not actually spoken to Beatrice, only listened to her messages reporting that all her friends were fine, that they had traveled safely through Tennessee, Arkansas, and Oklahoma, he just never thought of the possibility that they were in his company's vehicle. He thought she had rented a van from an agency in town since he knew she had been trying to make a reservation.

It wasn't until he saw James in church on Sunday that he learned the women had taken the missing vehicle. Jessie's husband happened to mention how nice it was of Dick to allow the women to drive it all the way to Texas to visit Margaret's people.

After the service, Dick called the local police department to tell them what had happened, but the description of the van had already been dispatched across the country, and even though Dick went through the appropriate channels to explain what had transpired, the stolen vehicle report had not been rescinded.

The deputies in Goodlett, Texas, had seen the van when it drove into town earlier that day. They were just up the road, parked in a small lot just where the speed limit changed from fifty-five miles per hour to thirty-five miles per hour, clocking incoming traffic. That was when they noticed the van and had witnessed what they described as erratic driving as it passed the Cotton Gin RV Park and then stopped abruptly, spun around, and headed back.

The two deputies had intended to follow the van and give the driver a warning or a ticket for reckless driving, but just as they pulled out of the lot, they had gotten a call that they were needed on the interstate as there had been a huge wreck in Childress.

They had managed to give a description of the van and report the number of the vehicle's license plate, requesting information, just before they were called away to the accident. Later, when they saw the van pull into the diner, the one deputy facing the parking lot remembered that he had not followed up on the call he made before he had been instructed to head over to Childress.

When he talked to the dispatcher to gather the information he had requested, just as he and his partner were finishing their meal, he discovered that the vehicle had been listed as stolen from North Carolina. And even though he thought it was a little odd that the thieves looked more like a group of grandmothers, one of whom was wearing a Santa hat, than hard-core criminals, he was sort of excited about apprehending car thieves. He was a new recruit to the sheriff's department, and it was to be his first arrest.

Once the women were surrounded by police cars and officers, ordered to put their hands on their heads, and then placed in custody in the rear section of the diner, Beatrice was allowed to call Dick. Another call was then placed from the police in Hope Springs, and everything was soon settled with the Goodlett sheriff. After the owner of the diner treated everyone to coffee and freshly baked apple pound cake that he was making for Christmas, everybody, including even the overzealous deputy, got a big kick out of what had happened.

There were all kinds of jokes made about strip searches and spending Christmas in a Texas jail, and Margaret was even able to meet a few of her very extended family members who had come over to the diner. Dick had chastised Beatrice so completely that even Louise didn't say anything else to her about what had happened.

By the time the women got back to their cabins, they were all exhausted. They fell into their beds wondering if the ice and snow would keep them in Goodlett for more than a couple of days, and wondering if everybody in town would soon know who they were and how they arrived.

It was early on Christmas Eve morning, an hour before the sun was expected to rise, that Margaret woke up. She was curious about the weather, and for some odd reason she couldn't explain, wanted to be outside.

She was quiet as she dressed in her warmest clothes, pulled the blanket around her, and headed out of the little cabin she shared with Jessie. She felt strangely alert, and everything about her felt vivid and clear in a way she hadn't noticed in many months. She felt somewhat energized, and the feeling surprised her.

The snow was falling. It looked like an inch or

two already covered the ground, and Margaret was relieved to discover that she did not detect any ice, just large, heavy flakes of snow. Even though the clouds filled the sky, there was a tiny sliver of a moon; and by its light, Margaret was able to see her way to the park office and to the short row of rocking chairs that stood along the rear wall facing the pool.

When she got to the chairs, she saw that someone was already sitting in one. She hesitated, not sure of who would be there, and then saw that it was Rachel, the young woman who had ridden with Charlotte from New Mexico. She was rocking, and she opened her eyes just as Margaret approached.

"Are you warm enough?" she asked the teenager and then sat in the chair beside her.

Rachel nodded and sat up a bit. She had a quilt wrapped around her, a wool cap on her head. "What time is it?" she asked.

"I'm not sure exactly," Margaret replied. "I guess around five o'clock maybe." She studied the young woman, surprised to find her out of the cabin. "How long have you been here?" she asked.

Rachel shrugged. "I think a couple of hours," she said. "I woke up and just couldn't sleep any more so I came out here to watch the snow."

"How long has it been coming down?" Margaret asked, pulling her blanket over her head and wrapping it tightly around her.

"It was just starting when I came out," she replied.

The two women sat silently. They both watched the sky, the thick flakes of snow glistening in the narrow moonlight. They heard a dog barking in the distance, the hooting of an old barn owl nearby.

"It's pretty, isn't it?" Margaret asked.

Rachel nodded. "I love snow," she remarked. "It was always real special when we got it here in Texas. We never had much."

"We didn't get a lot in North Carolina either. Some, more than now, but not like some parts of the country," Margaret responded.

"When I left Texas I saw a lot more of it in New Mexico. I think if I lived in a place where we didn't have it, I would miss it."

Margaret rocked a bit. The two women grew silent as a light wind blew around them. They bundled themselves even more inside their coverings.

"I never thought about it but I suppose snow will be something I miss too."

"Are you moving away?" Rachel asked. "Like to Florida or somewhere warm like that?"

Margaret seemed surprised. "Didn't Charlotte tell you?" she asked. She just assumed everyone knew that she was terminal. She thought it must have been tattooed across her forehead the way everyone treated her. She had felt the special attention, the avoidances, the greetings that went on too long, the heavy stares, for more than a month.

She simply figured that Charlotte would have told her young passenger why they were making this trip, why Margaret's skin had taken a yellow tint, why she was so fatigued. She simply assumed that the young woman, just a passerby on Margaret's short path of life, knew that she was going to die.

Rachel shook her head. "She just said that you were sick, that you had cancer, and that you were coming here to make peace with your family." She looked closely at the woman. "And I can tell that she cares a lot for you. She didn't have to tell me that."

Margaret smiled. "Yes, all of that is true." She thought about Charlotte, and her former pastor's discretion made her value their friendship even more.

She knew that lots of people would have thought they needed to explain a sick person's condition to a new person they would be meeting. They would have thought that it was necessary to use words like "terminal" or "vulnerable." She knew that lots of people would have wanted to use the travel time on the way to see a friend who was dying to talk about the impending death, what it would mean, how it would affect them.

Charlotte had apparently not done that. She had held confidence and not spoken of Margaret's condition even though there were no vows of confidentiality that would have been broken under these circumstances. The young pastor had always valued discretion. It had been one of the qualities that Margaret had appreciated the most.

"I'm dying," she confessed.

Rachel stopped rocking and sat up in her chair as if she was going to say something. But then she simply leaned back, the forward and backward sway of the chair maintaining a nice, easy rhythm.

"Do you hurt anywhere?" she asked.

Margaret looked over at the young woman. She found her questions innocent and refreshing. She did not mind at all the conversation she was having, even though she had thought she would be alone on this early Christmas Eve morning.

"My stomach hurts a little. The cancer is in my liver," she explained. "So sometimes after trying to digest a meal, I feel nauseated, sort of like how you feel when you have the flu."

Rachel nodded. "That's no fun," she responded.

"What about you?" Margaret asked. "You said that you had been in the hospital. Are you feeling better?"

"I was real bad for a while," she replied. "I thought I was dying. Well, actually, I think I was dying. I think I died even."

"Yeah?" Margaret asked.

"Yeah," Rachel replied.

"What was that like?"

"I didn't see no white light like everybody says," Rachel responded. "I was in the intensive care unit. I guess I had been in the hospital a couple of nights already but something happened and I could hear my machines going off and I felt all of the excitement going on in my room."

Margaret was listening attentively.

"There were lots of doctors and nurses all around my bed and it was like I floated above everything and watched them."

Margaret nodded. She had heard people who had gone through near-death experiences talk about that same kind of thing. She had heard them described as "out of body experiences."

"And I felt this kind of peace," Rachel explained. "But it wasn't like anything I had ever felt before." She hesitated.

"I used to do some drugs," she confessed, watching Margaret to see how she took the news. She saw that the woman didn't flinch or change anything about the way she was listening to her.

"Anyway, sometimes I would get this real relaxed feeling that I liked. I wouldn't care about anything but having this laid-back feeling." She shook her head. "But this peace I had when I watched them working on me, it wasn't anything like that."

Margaret nodded.

"It was like being in water and not having to hold your breath. Like the peace was just washing over you." She shook her head like she thought what she was saying sounded strange or unbelievable. "I guess that sounds pretty stupid, doesn't it?"

"No, not at all," Margaret responded. She glanced over at Rachel and then turned her head and looked up at the sky. She watched the snow as it fell into the empty pool.

"I sort of felt that way after my last surgery, when I was trying to decide whether or not to take any more treatments for my cancer. I had a dream kind of like that and I made the decision because of how I felt in that dream." She paused. "I felt like it was heaven. And I felt like I would be okay if I died."

Rachel smiled. "Yeah, that's how I felt too," she said, sounding very glad to meet and talk to someone who understood what she was saying, something she had never spoken to anyone because she worried that she would sound crazy.

"But you came back?" Margaret acknowledged.

Rachel nodded. "I did, but the truth is, I didn't want to." She thought about that night when her heart stopped, the night her body had crashed. "It was so nice," she added. "So perfectly quiet and restful and nice." She didn't have any other words to describe what had happened to her.

The two women sat in silence awhile, watching the snow, thinking about what happens beyond this world, how it is to die.

"So, what did you come back here for?" Margaret asked.

"I didn't have no choice. They stuffed this tube down my throat and shocked my heart until it started beating again."

Margaret smiled. "No, I mean to Texas." She looked over at the young woman and the two of them laughed a bit.

"Oh, I see," Rachel replied. Then she shrugged.

"This your home?" Margaret asked.

"Used to be. I grew up here. My sister is in Childress."

"Did you stop on your way here and see her?" Margaret asked.

Rachel shook her head. "I haven't decided if I'm going to visit her."

Margaret nodded. She chose not to ask the young woman anything further about her family situation. She knew that the way they had been talking, Rachel would share what she wanted to share, and that was already more than Margaret had expected.

"You got sisters?" Rachel asked.

Margaret nodded her head. "I have two sisters and two brothers but we're not very close," she explained. "They don't even know I'm this sick," she added. And then she decided to tell the young woman more than she had been asked. "Our mother died when we were all pretty young. I was just ten. They were teenagers mostly. And it seems like after she died, we just sort of drifted away from each other." She turned to Rachel. "Does that make sense?" she asked.

Rachel nodded. She thought about her own experience with her sister, how her sister had left Childress when their grandmother died, how Rachel had been angry with her since then and had not spoken to her in years.

"Is that why you're here, in Goodlett, I mean?" Rachel asked. "To see some of them and work it out?"

Margaret shook her head. "No, they're all back in North Carolina. And I think we made our peace with each other years ago about all of that. I guess that by the time I was an adult, I finally figured out that they weren't much older than I was when Mamma died and we were just trying to handle things the best way we could. We were all really young. Our dad was so heartbroken, he didn't have much for us and we just did what we knew how to do. So, no, I'm not really mad at any of them. We just sort of went down different paths but I'm not angry at them anymore."

"Are you angry at anybody?" Rachel asked.

Margaret thought about the question. She thought about the trip to Goodlett, what she was hoping to accomplish, what she was hoping to find. She knew that her friends had tried to ask the same question of her, wanted to try and figure out what this trip meant to her, but she had not been able to answer it. She had not really known why she needed to come to Goodlett, to be in her mother's hometown, until right at that moment.

And as the snow blanketed the little village that she had not visited since she was ten years old, that she had not seen except once, the Christmas before her mother died, Margaret understood that she had come there to relieve the burden of guilt she had placed upon her mother's ghost. She had come to Goodlett to forgive her mother for dying.

She considered Rachel's question and then simply shook her head.

"I was just a few days ago, just before we made this trip," she finally answered. "But now, in this light of moon and snow, I don't think I'm mad at anybody anymore."

# *Spicy Coffee Cake*

½ cup margarine
1 cup sugar
½ cup oil
2 cups flour
1 teaspoon baking soda
½ teaspoon salt
1 cup sour cream
1 teaspoon vanilla
⅓ cup brown sugar
½ cup sugar
1 teaspoon cinnamon
nuts, if desired

Cream together margarine, 1 cup sugar, and oil. Sift together flour, baking soda, and salt, and add to creamed mixture alternately with sour cream. Add vanilla. In separate bowl, combine brown sugar, ½ cup sugar, cinnamon, and nuts to make topping. Place half of cake batter in 9 x 13–inch greased and floured pan; add half of topping. Repeat. Bake at 350 degrees for 40 minutes.

# Chapter Twenty

By the time the sun rose on Christmas Eve in Goodlett, Texas, the snow was no longer falling and the ground was covered in a deep, white blanket. The women got up early, dressed, and enjoyed a spicy coffee cake, made for them by Maurice's wife, who was working that morning in the office. In return, they gave her one of their new cake cookbooks. They had only a couple left after dispersing them in restaurants and hotels and rest areas all along the interstate.

Jessie and Louise and Beatrice sat in the small outer room where a fire was burning and enjoyed their breakfast while Rachel went into the small back office and used the phone to call her sister. They all noticed that she seemed to be gone for a long time.

Maurice drove Margaret and Charlotte over to the church in his pickup truck and waited for them as the two women walked to the cemetery and found Margaret's mother's grave.

Charlotte stood next to her friend as she placed a small peace lily against the headstone. The plant had been a gift from Jessie, something she had managed to hide from Margaret after purchasing it at a small florist in Oklahoma.

Jessie had given it to Margaret Christmas Eve

morning when she and Charlotte were getting ready to go to the cemetery.

"I thought you might like something to leave with her," Jessie said, and gave her the small potted plant, the leaves sturdy and glossy green.

They all knew the plant would probably never survive in the cold wintry blast they were experiencing, but Margaret didn't really worry about the plant.

"It's perfect," she told Jessie, understanding the meaning behind the plant's name as much as the purpose for the gift. "I have made my peace," she added.

Charlotte stood watching as Margaret placed the plant on the grave and then quietly waited until her friend finished and then came to stand beside her.

"I want you to know that you're the reason I came to do this," Margaret said to Charlotte.

The young woman turned to her, surprised at the comment. "Me, why?" she asked.

"It was the photograph you sent me when you first moved to New Mexico," she explained. "It was the one where I told you that you looked like you had fallen in love."

Charlotte smiled. She remembered the photograph and the conversation.

"You told me that since you moved out west that you felt the most like yourself you ever had." Margaret took her by the hand. "Do you remember that?" she asked.

Charlotte nodded but gave no reply.

"I knew that I hadn't felt like that in a long time. That here I was, almost seventy years old, and I couldn't remember what it was to feel that much at peace, that much like myself, a self that isn't sullied by emotional baggage or distracted by silly things, old broken things. I realized then that I hadn't felt that way since I was ten years old, a little girl here in this place, sitting next to my mother, who was saying good-bye to me, only I didn't know it."

Charlotte dropped her face, her chin nestled inside her scarf.

"I carried bitterness around for sixty years like it was something I had to strap on my back and take with me. I was so mad at her for sending us back to North Carolina, for staying here, for dying." Margaret looked at the grave, her mother's headstone.

"You never seemed bitter to me," Charlotte noted. "I never knew you carried this stuff around with you. You're one of the most put-together women I know."

"Well, I guess if one has from the time they are ten years old to figure out how to package the anger or sadness in a way that it can be integrated into life, it's easy to keep it well-hidden, even unnoticed by very good friends."

"That's the gift of dying, I think." Margaret looked up at the bright blue sky, the sun melting the frozen earth.

"What's that?" Charlotte asked.

"That you get to take an honest inventory of everything. There's no pretending that things are more or less than what they are. You go through everything that matters, the memories, the dreams, the regrets, the friendships, and you get the chance to revisit everything you want to, everything you've put off your whole life looking at. And that's when you finally figure out what you've held on to the tightest. What you need finally to let go."

Charlotte glanced at all the graves around her and wondered how many of the dead had used their last days, their last moments, to do what Margaret had done.

"I was angry at my mother for a very long time. I forgave my brothers and sisters for falling away, but it never occurred to me that I was mad at her for the same thing. It just never dawned on me that she was only doing what a mother does. She was just trying to do the best for her children, trying to protect us the way any mother would do, trying to keep us from death."

Margaret shook her head and blew out a long breath.

"Sixty years is a long time to wrap a heart up in sorrow. It's a long time to be mad." She squeezed Charlotte's hand. "But at least I know now, at least I found my way back to Goodlett, back to her."

Charlotte nodded and turned to face her friend.

Margaret was relaxed in a way the young pastor had never seen her. There was a peace about her she had never even suspected was missing.

"And you look just like yourself," Charlotte said.

The two women hugged and headed back to Maurice's truck.

By lunchtime the snow had melted and Margaret announced that she wanted to go back to Hope Springs. She wanted, in fact, if such a thing was possible, to be home by dinnertime the next night.

Jessie and Beatrice immediately understood that she was hurrying the return trip because she thought her friends should be with their families for Christmas, and even though they tried to talk her out of it, her mind was made up. Her Christmas wish, she told them, had been fulfilled, and now, she said, she wanted to go home so that they could have theirs too.

After Beatrice heard from Dick that the van was needed by the funeral home before the end of the week, and once they heard the latest weather report that another storm was fast approaching from the west, they decided that if they left at lunchtime and drove in shifts straight through the night, they would, in fact, be home by Christmas evening.

Charlotte chose to go back with them, thinking that she could help with the driving and that it would give her the opportunity to visit her mother and a few friends in Hope Springs. Maurice told her that she could leave her car in Goodlett, there at the park, and if necessary, she could fly into Amarillo and he would arrange to get it to the airport. Charlotte could also see that Margaret was nearing the end, and she wanted to be with her during her last days. She knew that Maria was handling things at the shelter and everything would be fine while she was away.

Rachel was able to contact her sister and was helping the women pack up the van when an old brown station wagon came driving down the highway. They all watched as it pulled into the parking lot and then as a young woman, a spitting image of Rachel, opened the door and got out.

"That her?" Charlotte asked, as she was standing right next to the young woman.

Rachel nodded and watched as her sister stood at the car. Neither of them seemed to know what to do.

Rachel glanced around, trying to find Margaret. When Rachel caught her eye, the older woman winked at her. The two smiled at each other, and Rachel nodded. It was a private conversation the two of them had already had. There was nothing left for them to say to each other.

"I'll come back and get you if you want," Charlotte noted.

Rachel shook her head and smiled. "I got a job here at the park," she explained.

The women glanced around at one another, wondering when that transaction had occurred.

"I'm going to run the place while they go on vacation." Then she grinned. "I talked on the phone to Ricky this morning, with his mother. He'll be home in the summer," she added.

Charlotte lifted her eyebrows as if she was pleased and surprised at the announcement.

"And besides," the young woman said as she looked back over in her sister's direction, "this is home." And with that, she took her bag that Charlotte was holding and walked toward the car that was waiting for her.

They all watched as the two young women stood across from each other for a brief second and then finally embraced. Rachel waved as they pulled out of the parking lot and onto the road.

"Well, I just hope she slows down before she runs into our deputy friend," Beatrice said as she continued loading the back. "Is that everything?" she asked.

And they all got into the van.

The women left Texas and drove for more than twenty hours across Oklahoma, Arkansas, Tennessee, and finally into North Carolina. Louise took the first shift, then Jessie. Charlotte drove through most of the night, with each of them taking turns keeping the driver awake. They sang Christmas carols, played word games, stopped to eat a number of times, laughed about stolen vans, and considered out loud whether they would ever be welcome again at Graceland.

Margaret slept for most of the trip, and they all noticed that there was a new rattle in her breathing, that there was something, even though they couldn't name it, that had changed about their friend's condition. They did not mention this as the reason but they all drove even harder, trying to get Margaret home and comfortable as quickly as they could.

Beatrice was at the wheel again Christmas morning when they finally rolled into Hope Springs. They were tired by the time they got home and no one was really talking too much. They were taking Jessie home first when Louise caught sight of something going on at the church.

"Was there a service there this morning?" she asked.

Beatrice slowed down as they turned on the street that went right past the church and Jessie's house.

Jessie shook her head. "No, that was just last night."

All of them saw that the parking lot was full of cars and that several television news trucks and crews were standing in the driveway. Beatrice inched forward as she spotted the police cars and saw the lights flashing. She thought about pulling away as quickly as possible, thinking that the report of the stolen van was the reason behind all the commotion at the church.

"There's a limousine parked out front," Charlotte noted. "Maybe there's a funeral."

The women all turned to Beatrice, wondering if Dick had mentioned a death in the community to her. Just as she was about to explain that she didn't know anything about a service scheduled for Christmas Day, she saw James waving at them from the edge of the church property. She slowed down just as she got beside him and pulled off the road. Jessie rolled down her window as he ran toward them.

"What's going on?" she asked her husband. "And man, I'm glad to see you!"

"I'm glad to see you too!"

They clasped hands. "Merry Christmas, everybody," he said. And then he saw Charlotte. "Well, look what you found in Texas!" He glanced around and saw Margaret sleeping in the back.

"Hey James," Charlotte said.

"What's going on?" Beatrice asked. "What's happening at the church?"

"Well, Beatrice, you have really done it this time," James said loudly.

Beatrice sighed and put both hands on the steering wheel in a gesture of surrender. "I know that I forgot to tell Dick about the van," she said, as she reached over and shifted the vehicle in park. "I know what I did. And I am really sorry about it," she added. "But I thought this was all cleared up." She dropped her head, and the Santa cap fell off in her lap.

The women could see the news crews running toward them. Beatrice ducked down in her seat.

"No, Bea!" James exclaimed. "It's that Cake Lady from New York. She's come here to announce the winner of the cake contest."

And it was then that the crowds descended upon the women parked in the funeral van just beside the church driveway. Beatrice finally got out after she began to be questioned by a reporter. She didn't really want the van shown on camera. She pushed at the sides of her hair and smoothed down the front of her pants.

Louise and Jessie and Charlotte watched all the excitement from the van while Margaret continued to sleep. The Cake Lady waved at them from her limousine as she pulled away.

"We have with us now Beatrice Witherspoon, the project coordinator for the recipe contest idea." The young reporter turned to Beatrice and asked, "Since this was your idea, what do you think about the winning recipe?" She stuck her microphone in Beatrice's face.

Beatrice looked around nervously, not knowing how to respond. That was when she saw the police escorting a man back to the police car. The man smiled and waved at Beatrice, revealing a big blue ribbon in his hands and a pair of handcuffs around his wrists. Beatrice then understood that the prison inmate, the creator of the lemon lavender pound cake, had been selected as the winner by the famous chef. She grinned and waved at him and felt a huge sigh of relief that the police cars were there because of him and not because of her recent theft of a funeral van.

She also glanced around and noticed Betty Mills standing with a small crowd on the front lawn of the church. Beatrice held her head very high and began to answer the questions given to her by the reporter.

Later the entire interview with Beatrice was on the evening news as well as in the paper the next day. There was also a big story about the famous pastry chef from New York who had flown in just to make her announcement that the lemon lavender pound cake was her choice for the Hope Springs Christmas Cake.

After making sure they got good television and media coverage, the Cake Lady was back on a plane heading north. Apparently she was in need of some good public relations because of a mishap with some movie star's birthday cake. She had put a big number 45 on the cake in honor of the age of the star, only to find out the famous actor had been telling everyone she was only thirty-nine.

The Cake Lady was desperate for some act of goodwill they could exploit, and once they were discussing options, her assistant had remembered all the phone calls made by a woman and some cake contest in a little town down south. Once they got all the specifics, the staff agreed that this was the perfect solution. They tried unsuccessfully to reach the woman who had contacted them. So the staff and crew simply contacted the local newspapers and television stations and showed up on Christmas Day to announce the winner.

The fact that the Cake Lady's favorite recipe had been sent in by an inmate in prison seemed to add just the right flavor that her publicist had been seeking. The Cake Lady was able to talk about her concern for those in prison and even how she was considering taping a few of her cooking show episodes from prison kitchens. It had all turned out perfectly.

Once the media circus was over, Beatrice went home. Dick forgave her for taking the van, and they enjoyed a quiet dinner at home. They had been invited to his cousin's house, and even though Beatrice considered how much she would enjoy watching Betty eat a little crow, she knew where she wanted to be later in the evening.

After dropping Jessie off to change and spend a little time with James and her family, Louise and Charlotte took Margaret home. They helped her as she walked into her house. She was surprised and pleased that Frances Martin had arranged to have a small tree delivered and placed near the front of the house, so that everything seemed joyful and festive.

Louise helped Margaret get changed and ready for bed as Charlotte fixed hot tea. They called the hospice nurse, who came over and assessed the situation and adjusted Margaret's pain medicine. The nurse didn't say much to the two women with her patient; she could see that they understood what was happening. She could see that they would be fine and left her number in case they needed her.

It was about midnight, hours after Jessie and Beatrice had joined their friends to sit around Margaret's bed, that she died.

Before she passed, they sang a few songs and told the stories they loved most about Margaret, stories from years and years of friendship. Charlotte told them that Margaret had taught her as much about living as she had about dying and that she had never met anyone who was always so clear about what was the right thing to do.

Louise seemed to have the hardest time with letting go, but by the time the moment came, even she knew it was right and was able to let her friend pass in peace.

They were silent when she left. They had said everything they needed to say to the woman they loved. They had told her they would be fine without her, even though they weren't completely sure they believed it. They had promised her that they would look after one another and hold one another accountable in their relationships. And Beatrice, with a wink, had even made sure to promise to Margaret that they would all see that Charlotte got married.

This last statement had made them laugh their last laugh, there around Margaret's bed. And just as Christmas faded into another day, the Hope Springs Church Cookbook Committee grieved and celebrated the life of one they cherished. They said good-bye to Margaret, understanding that the greatest miracle they had known was the miracle of how they had learned to love enough to let one of their own go in peace.

# Reading Group Guide

1. As in previous situations, Beatrice talks her friends into taking on a project to try to take their minds off Margaret's cancer. Do you think this is an effective way to cope with a tragedy in your life? Have you ever been involved in what felt like a "diversion project"?

2. Margaret and Charlotte have a special bond, as friends and as parishioner and minister. Have you ever felt particularly close to someone who played a role in your life like that of a minister? If so, what did that relationship mean to you?

3. In a phone conversation between Margaret and Charlotte, Charlotte explains that "I feel like myself" in the Southwest. "It's like I've come to a place of perfect peace." Do you feel this is true of the place where you live now? If not, is there another place where you feel this way?

4. Charlotte works in a battered women's shelter in Gallup, New Mexico. Why do you think she left Hope Springs to take this job? How is it similar to or different from her work as a parish minister?

5. Although Charlotte is far away from Margaret, she does her best to help her sick friend. Have you ever been geographically distant from someone who needed your support? How did you handle it? What do you think a friend should do in this situation?

6. After some denial, Beatrice finally admits that she suffers from depression. Why do you think she became depressed? What were her symptoms? What do you think she should have done to get help?

7. Margaret decides that she needs to get back to Texas to find her mother's family. Why do you think this trip is important to Margaret? Do you feel that she is able to get what she wants from the trip?

8. Rachel is a teenager and Margaret is an older woman, but they still are able to find some things in common with each other. How would you characterize their relationship? What are they able to learn from each other?

9. How does Margaret think of death? What does she see as the "gift of dying"? Do you agree with this view of death? Why or why not?

10. James points out to Jessie that friends, true friends, are rare and wonderful. How do the women in this book show their friendship to one another through difficult times? Who are your true friends, and what makes them special for you?

**LYNNE HINTON** is the pastor of St. Paul's United Church of Christ in Rio Rancho, New Mexico. The author of numerous novels including *Friendship Cake*, *Hope Springs*, *Forever Friends*, *Christmas Cake*, and *Wedding Cake*, she lives in Albuquerque, New Mexico.

www.lynnehinton.com

**Center Point Publishing**
600 Brooks Road • PO Box 1
Thorndike ME 04986-0001 USA

**(207) 568-3717**

**US & Canada:**
**1 800 929-9108**
www.centerpointlargeprint.com